"I'll sign the divorce papers on one condition, Lacey."

Devin took a deep breath. "You stay here at the ranch until the babies are born. Afterward, if you still want me to, I'll sign."

"Devin, I have a life—a family—in Oklahoma. I have to go home." Lacey pushed to her feet. "It's a wild idea."

"It probably is, but that's the deal." Devin forced himself to relax.

"You know I could take you to court anyway."

"I know, but I'm really hoping you won't. Give me a chance to show you that I can be a better person. That I can be a man who'll show up for his family. If you don't stay, you'll never know."

There were twin spots of color high on Lacey's cheekbones. "I need some time to think about this."

"You can have all the time you need."

Devin prayed that once she gave it some thought, she would want to stay. And he would have a second chance…

Award-winning author **Stephanie Dees** lives in small-town Alabama with her pastor husband and two youngest children. A Southern girl through and through, she loves sweet tea, SEC football, corn on the cob and air-conditioning. For further information, please visit her website at stephaniedees.com.

Books by Stephanie Dees

Love Inspired

Triple Creek Cowboys
The Cowboy's Twin Surprise

Family Blessings
The Dad Next Door
A Baby for the Doctor
Their Secret Baby Bond
The Marriage Bargain

Visit the Author Profile page at Harlequin.com for more titles.

The Cowboy's Twin Surprise

Stephanie Dees

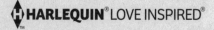

HARLEQUIN® LOVE INSPIRED®

Recycling programs
for this product may
not exist in your area.

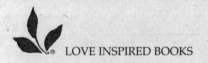

LOVE INSPIRED BOOKS

ISBN-13: 978-1-335-53937-3

The Cowboy's Twin Surprise

Copyright © 2019 by Stephanie Newton

www.Harlequin.com

Printed in U.S.A.

And he said unto me, My grace is sufficient
for thee: for my strength is made perfect in
weakness. Most gladly therefore will I
rather glory in my infirmities, that
the power of Christ may rest upon me.
—*2 Corinthians* 12:9

For Riley. Thanks for always encouraging me to be my best self and for loving me even when I'm not. Being your mom is a privilege.

Acknowledgments

A book is never a solitary endeavor, and so many people helped me along the way with this book. Thanks to Melissa Jeglinski and Melissa Endlich for believing in this story and helping me define it.

Thanks to my critique partner, Sierra Donovan, and best beta reader evah, Janet Sallis. And a special thanks to those people who propped me up when I needed a friend, an ear or an idea bouncer: Sarah Kate Newton, Brenda Minton, Tina Radcliffe. You're irreplaceable.

Chapter One

Devin Cole let his truck roll to a stop at the end of the lane, just short of the driveway to the family ranch. He slid his Narcotics Anonymous newcomers coin between his fingers and back again. He was measuring his life in days and hours now…moments, maybe. One hour since his last meeting. Six days out of rehab. Thirty-six days clean. Thirty-nine days and seven hours since he'd stopped running from God.

Forty days since he'd messed things up with Lacey—the only friend he'd managed to keep on his not-so-slow slide into recklessness and addiction. It had been a long time since his Sunday school days, but in the Bible, wasn't it always forty days that people spent in the wilderness?

A warm breeze wafted through the open window, bringing with it the scent of freshly turned dirt and ribs in the smoker. The sound of calves in the field. Springtime in Alabama.

His eyes went from the farmhouse peeking through the trees to linger on the white welcome chip sliding through his fingers. Chances were pretty good he'd gotten a better welcome from NA than he'd get from his brothers.

Unfortunately, his options were limited. As in, he didn't have any. After he'd shattered his ankle, his days in the rodeo were over. He'd tried to continue, relying more and more on prescriptions and alcohol to fight through the pain. But he'd failed. Failed his corporate sponsors. Failed his friends and family. And most of all failed himself.

He'd spent the past six days and his last thousand bucks driving cross-country, trying to make amends for the wrongs he'd done. And he'd learned apologies went only so far to repair burned bridges.

He put his old truck in gear and drove the rest of the way to the house. Even in the waning daylight, the white two-story clapboard looked a little more worn than it had the last time he'd seen it, the sunny yellow porch swing peeling and faded. No cheery flowers filled the beds that lined the walkway.

The screen door opened and his older brother Tanner stepped out in his dusty boots. Right away, Devin knew from the look in Tanner's eyes this wasn't going to be a prodigal son welcome. No warm embraces. No parties thrown on his behalf. He nodded, to himself, mostly. A firm let's-get-on-with-it nod.

Devin picked up the cane he had to use now that his pain wasn't dulled by drugs. He slid off the old leather seat, relief flooding his body when his feet touched the ground.

Home.

Tanner's blue eyes searched Devin's for signs that he was using, and Devin felt a pang of regret. With a barely suppressed sigh, Tanner pulled the door open wide. "Come on in. I've got coffee on."

Devin followed his brother into the farmhouse, noting the threadbare rug on the floor and the worn leather couch, still the same one from when they were kids. Although they'd never been wealthy, they'd gotten by, but now… It almost seemed that the ranch had aged ten years in the three since he'd seen it.

With a practiced economy of movement,

Tanner took two mugs from the cabinet by the sink and filled them with coffee. "What happened to the big fancy truck you were driving last time you were here?"

"Sold it to pay for rehab."

Tanner's eyes flicked to his. "And your horse?"

"Left her with Lacey."

A dark eyebrow quirked. "Another debt?"

"You could say that." A memory of a brown-eyed girl with laughter in her eyes flashed in his mind. Devin took a swig of the coffee and suppressed the wish for something stronger. Because running from uncomfortable emotions was how he got himself in this mess in the first place, or at least that was what the counselor at rehab told him.

The fatigue of the last six weeks pulled hard at him. He took off his ball cap and scrubbed a hand through hair that could use a good trim. "I'm sorry, Tanner. I don't even know where to start to say how sorry I am."

Tanner still didn't smile. "What do you want, Devin?"

"I want to come home."

At his brother's sharply expelled breath, Devin started to panic, just a little. "You sacrificed a lot for me. I know that. And I wasted the opportunities."

After their parents died, Tanner had finished the job of raising him. He'd scrimped and saved and bought Devin his first cutting horse. He'd been at every event from the first to the time Devin kicked loose of Red Hill Springs and everyone in it.

Tanner crossed his arms. "If you're wanting me to argue with you about that, you're gonna be waiting a long time."

His hat literally in his hands, Devin closed his eyes and sent a wordless prayer toward Heaven before he opened them again and looked Tanner in the eyes. "I'm an addict. I'll always be an addict, but I don't have to be a bad person. Please give me a chance to prove I can do better."

"We've been down this road before."

Devin went still. There was nothing he could say or do to change his brother's mind. Because Tanner was right. It was a familiar refrain from his teenage years—even before the drugs, Devin had struggled. They *had* been down this road before where Devin had begged and pleaded and unfailingly messed things up. So he waited and he wondered if there was anyone left who would take him in until he could find a job.

Tanner didn't tap his foot or jiggle his leg or any of the things normal people did. He simply stared into the black coffee in his cup until he reached a decision. He looked up. "I could use the help around here."

Devin let out all his anxiety in one pent-up breath.

His brother held up a finger. "But there are ground rules, Dev, and if you break them, there are no second chances."

In the past, Devin would've brushed aside the bit about the rules. Ground rules were for boring people who didn't have any fun. Now, Devin was clinging to the rules by his fingernails, just to hold on to his sobriety. He asked Tanner quietly, "What do you want me to do?"

"One. You go to meetings every day. Two. You always tell me where you're going to be. Three. There are no rock stars at Triple Creek Ranch. You pull your own weight."

It didn't sound like much but Devin knew from experience that pulling his weight around the ranch was a full-time job. Working the farm was going to be hard with his injury but it wouldn't be impossible.

He could promise Tanner that he was different, that he'd matured past the kid who'd looked for approval in all the wrong places, but promises didn't mean much. He wanted more than anything to prove to his brother that he could change. To prove to himself that he could be more than just some rodeo guy who partied a lot and nearly got himself killed. He said quietly, "Thanks, Tanner."

"Don't make me regret this, Devin." The man who'd started raising Devin when he was still practically a boy himself had a world of disappointment in his eyes. He jerked a thumb at the stairs. "You can have your old room."

Devin nodded. He pushed back from the table and limped onto the porch of the farmhouse. He'd run far and fast away from here when he'd turned eighteen, too big for these parts. Maybe it was fitting that when there was nothing left of him, he ran home. If he was lucky, maybe it was here that he'd find all the pieces of himself he'd lost along the way.

Two months later

Lacey Jenkins checked her GPS one last time as she drove through Red Hill Springs,

Alabama. The flower boxes that lined the street were filled with geraniums, and American flags on the lampposts fluttered in the wind. All decked out for the upcoming Memorial Day holiday, the town was adorable, but she wasn't having it. She'd been stewing for three and a half months now, ever since she'd woken up alone in a hotel room in Vegas, ink barely dry on a quickie marriage certificate proclaiming her married to rodeo superstar Devin Cole.

She should've listened to the voice of warning in her head—the one that sounded strangely like her dad, coaching her around the barrels when she was a kid. "Ride from here, Lacey-girl," he'd say, as he tapped his forehead under the brim of his cowboy hat. "Not from here" as he tapped his heart. "The heart will betray you. The head will lead you." But she'd been caught up in the adventure of it all. The romance. She and Devin had been friends—best friends—for years, even as he seemed to get more and more reckless. That weekend in Vegas after the rodeo competition ended, he'd seemed more like his old self. Sweeter and more thoughtful than he'd been in a while.

Until he'd disappeared the morning after

they'd gotten married. And then, a month later, he'd had the nerve to drop off his horse for her like some kind of consolation prize.

So yeah, if she'd been mad before, now she was boiling. He'd left her *and* he'd left his horse.

Her GPS calmly announced that she'd arrived at her destination. Nerves fluttered in her stomach, a fact she noted with some irritation. She was a world champion barrel racer. She was supposed to be immune to nerves.

Turning into the drive at the farmhouse, she slowed to look around. She had the right address, but this didn't look anything like the bustling ranch she'd imagined as Devin had talked about it back when they were still friends. But still, there was a sunny yellow swing on the front porch with a fresh coat of paint and brightly colored zinnias filling the flower beds in front of the house.

She eased her truck to a stop so Reggie wouldn't be jostled. The big horse had been patient for the duration of the long trip, but he had to be as antsy as she was to get out of the truck after days on the road. She stepped out onto the gravel drive, pressing a hand into her lower back and leaning into a stretch.

It had taken her a full two days to get here, and once she set a few things straight with Devin, she'd be turning right around to go back.

Lacey reached for a file of papers she'd left on the passenger side of the truck, and when she turned back around she was eye level with three sets of well-worn boots. Her gaze skimmed the length of long denim-clad legs and stalled out at the world champion rodeo buckle at the waist of the jeans on the right before continuing upward to meet three identical sets of dark brown eyes.

She gulped. The Cole brothers were unilaterally staring at her, and to be honest, it was a little bit intimidating. But at least she knew she was in the right place.

Lacey flicked a glance at the one standing on the left side of Devin—the oldest brother, Tanner, she thought—and saw his unsmiling eyes travel from her to Devin and back again. Dark hair curled underneath a faded red ball cap. He settled it a little farther on his head and continued to stare at her.

She swallowed hard as her vision grayed around the edges. Wow. She must be more tired than she thought she was.

"Lacey? What are you doing here?" Devin's

words sliced through her exhaustion and, despite girding herself with all that anger, they still had the power to hurt her.

She looked Devin Cole right in the eyes and said, "I want a divorce."

The color drained from Devin's face, and she felt a perverse pleasure that she'd managed to shock him.

"Divorce?" The other brother's head snapped straight. "You're *married*?"

Devin remained unnaturally still.

"I'll just unload Reggie, then." Tanner shifted away as if the tension strung between Lacey and Devin would snap under the pressure. He clambered down from the porch and lowered the back of the trailer. She could hear his voice as he spoke softly to Devin's cutting horse, backing him gently down the ramp.

Devin's gaze never broke with Lacey's, but he said, "Garrett, feel free to move along anytime."

The middle brother, with a mop of unruly dark curls and studious-looking glasses, shook his head. "Nope. Uh-uh. Sounds like you need legal representation. I'm not going anywhere." He grinned. "Plus, I wouldn't miss this for anything."

Lacey refused to be the first one to look

away. But her head was spinning again, her husband's handsome, serious face swimming before her eyes. She groped blindly behind her for the side of the truck, her file of papers slipping from her fingers to scatter on the ground.

The last thing she saw before she crumpled was the fear on Devin's face as he dropped his cane and leaped down the stairs, his strong arms scooping her up just before she hit the ground.

Devin lifted Lacey into his arms, concern for her blocking out all other thoughts. "Garrett, get a doctor out here."

"Want me to call an ambulance?"

"No, she's terrified of hospitals. Just call someone. Please?" Devin carried Lacey up the porch steps. He managed to pull the screen door slightly ajar and kick it open. Her face was pale—too pale—against the dark shine of her hair.

He laid her gently on the wide leather couch, heart thudding in his chest. "Lace? Come on, girl, you gotta wake up. You're scaring me."

Just when he thought he'd made peace with

the things he'd done when he was using, she showed up with this gem. *Married?*

He didn't really question what he'd been thinking, but what had *she* been thinking marrying him? The last thing Lacey needed was to be married to a washed-up rodeo cowboy with a drug-addiction problem.

Especially one who didn't even remember their wedding even happened.

Of all the stupid things he'd done that he didn't remember, destroying his relationship with Lacey was the worst. She was the best thing that ever happened to him and he'd screwed it up, along with the rest of his life.

But marriage? He couldn't even fathom it.

"Come on, Lacey, wake up. I know you still have a few things to say to me."

Garrett stepped quietly in the door, his cell phone and a bunch of papers in his hand. "Ash Sheehan is on his way."

Devin stabbed his fingers into his hair, worry settling into his shoulders like thousand-pound weights. "Isn't he a kids' doctor?"

"Yeah. He's also the only doctor in town. We can take her to the hospital, Dev. It's probably what Ash is going to tell us to do anyway."

"I can't." Devin dropped on the coffee table

in front of the couch, his ruined ankle aching now that the adrenaline had faded. He studied Lacey's still form on the couch. Color was slowly returning to her face. "She'd kill me."

"She dropped these when she fainted." Garrett slid the papers onto the table beside Devin and placed his cane within easy reach. "Tanner's getting Reggie settled. I'm gonna go make some coffee. I have a feeling we're going to need it."

Garrett disappeared into the kitchen, and Devin glanced down at the papers.

There was a legal-looking stack, which he assumed was the divorce papers she wanted him to sign. He picked them up and glanced at the first paragraph before tossing them aside. As he did, another piece of paper fluttered to the ground. He leaned over and picked up the flimsy grainy black-and-white photo.

His skin went clammy.

He knew what this was. It was a still from an ultrasound. And this one had two arrows pointing at two tiny peanut-shaped blobs. He dropped the photo like it was on fire.

Was Lacey *pregnant*?

Chapter Two

Devin scratched his head, his mind trying to make sense of what he'd just seen. Could Lacey really be expecting? *Twins?*

He glanced at her stomach, but it didn't look any different to him from how it always had. Maybe a little rounder. He studied her face. Maybe it was a little fuller? Her long dark hair curled past her shoulders, framing a peaches-and-cream complexion.

She was so beautiful. Always had been.

And in that second he imagined her holding two babies. Their babies. A tsunami of longing washed over him. It was a dream that seemed so far out of reach for someone like him.

He picked the photo up again. Sure enough, her name was written at the top of the image.

Lacey Cole. Seeing it in print was a punch to the gut.

Lacey really was pregnant.

Devin scrubbed his hands over his face. He remembered waking up in Vegas and seeing Lacey lying in his bed. Realizing that, with one monumentally horrible decision in a string of really bad decisions, he'd managed to mess up the one thing he still really cared about.

That moment had changed his life.

Her eyes fluttered open and slowly focused. Devin saw the instant she remembered what happened. She tried to sit up, arms flailing, pupils dilating in panic.

He grabbed her shoulders, forcing her to focus on him. "Lacey, you're at Triple Creek Ranch."

When she looked confused, he said, "You brought Reggie home and you told me you want a divorce."

Her voice was a little hoarse and husky when she said, "Well, at least we got that out of the way."

The corner of his mouth twitched up. The bone-deep fear faded a little bit, but he was left with so many questions and no answers to speak of. "Seems like a pretty good call.

I mean, honestly, what were you thinking, marrying someone like me in the first place?"

Hurt flared in her eyes, but she blinked it away. Tension still vibrated in her muscles, but she'd stopped trying to get away from him. "Clearly, I wasn't thinking at all. Did you call anyone?"

He shook his head, knowing immediately what she wanted to know. "No EMTs. I know the rules. No hospital unless you're gushing blood from an artery or some other equally dire circumstance."

Her shoulders relaxed under his fingers and she let out the breath she'd been holding. "Thank you."

"You're welcome." He dropped his hands, clenching his fingers slowly into fists. He wanted to grab the ultrasound photo, shove it in her face and demand she talk to him. *Is this yours?*

Are they mine?

Instead, he uncoiled his fingers one by one until he felt in control again. "You gave us a scare. Are you feeling okay?"

Well, that was a dumb question. Of course she wasn't feeling okay. She'd just passed out in his front yard.

He was saved by a knock at the door. He

jumped to his feet and nearly fell over as his stupid ankle gave out on him. Lacey didn't say anything but he could feel her curiosity as he hobbled to the door.

Ash Sheehan entered the room with an old-fashioned black doctor's satchel. He shook Devin's hand and crossed immediately to the couch. "I'm Dr. Sheehan. Garrett called me."

"I'm Lacey… Jenkins." Her eyes cut to Devin but quickly flitted back to the doctor, who didn't look anything like the octogenarian Devin had been expecting to see at the door. "Thank you for coming."

"Most of the time I see patients under the age of eighteen, so you'll have to be patient with me." Ash pulled a blood pressure cuff out of his bag and smiled, his blue eyes warming on Lacey's.

He looked like something out of a fashion ad. Devin wanted to punch him in the face.

Wrapping the cuff around her arm and tucking the stethoscope earpieces into his ears, Ash said, "So Garrett told me on the phone that you fainted a little while ago. Is this the first time something like this has happened?"

Lacey's gaze drifted to Devin again. He sighed. "I'll just be in the kitchen."

He glanced at his cane, leaning on the coffee table. He wanted more than anything to ignore it and stride into the kitchen like a man who wasn't hanging on to ninety-four days of sobriety minute by minute.

Lacey deserved better. But Devin owed it to her—and himself—not to hide anymore.

Lacey watched Devin limp into the kitchen, leaning heavily on a cane. She knew he'd shattered his ankle. Everyone knew that. It had happened on live TV. But he hadn't been using a cane the last time she'd seen him. He'd only been slightly favoring one ankle, if at all.

He'd seemed so shocked when she said she wanted a divorce. And suddenly she'd felt cold and hot and her head was spinning and she'd wondered for the first time if he even remembered they got married.

She wondered the same thing now. He hadn't seemed high that weekend in Vegas, but once she heard from mutual friends that he'd spent a month in rehab, she'd started to understand just how good he'd become at hiding it.

Well, whether he remembered their wedding or not, he'd left her without a word. That was the part she'd found unbearable. And now? It wasn't just her own heart she had to protect.

Dr. Sheehan pulled the earpieces of his stethoscope out of his ears and unstrapped her arm from the blood pressure cuff. "So I assume from your reaction earlier that this isn't the first time you've passed out?"

She sighed, her hand creeping to her stomach. "No. It's happened a couple of other times but it's been a few weeks. I thought it had passed."

"Your blood pressure's pretty low. Any history of that being an issue?"

She glanced at the kitchen and lowered her voice. "Only since I've been pregnant. I'm fourteen weeks pregnant with twins."

"Congratulations." The handsome doctor smiled. "I have a new baby myself. So, Garrett said you just drove in from Oklahoma? You were obviously sitting a lot on the trip. Did you sleep?"

She looked away. "A little, here and there."

"Okay." The doctor coiled his stethoscope around his palm and placed it back in his bag. "Are you having any pain?"

"Mild cramps. My OB in Oklahoma said it was normal, especially with twins."

Dr. Sheehan nodded. "It can be. Anything else going on? Fever? Any other aches and pains?"

She shook her head.

"I think between the low blood pressure, the demands on your body of early pregnancy and your long trip, you've just hit your limit. I also think you should see an obstetrician as soon as possible."

"When I get home, I promise I'll see my regular doctor and then I'll put my feet up for the next six months."

"Yeah, about that…" He didn't smile, which was her first inkling that she wasn't going to like what he had to say. "My medical advice would be not to plan to go anywhere for a while. You're carrying twins, which makes this a higher-risk pregnancy. If you were my wife or sister, I'd suggest you plan to stay here for at least a month, for your sake and the health of the babies. I'll refer you to an OB in Mobile and you can get a thorough workup before you try to make that trip cross-country again."

His face was kind as he shattered her plans, so at least there was that. Her eyes filled with tears anyway. "Thanks, Dr. Sheehan."

"Please call me Ash. This wasn't an official visit, just a favor for a friend." His eyes crinkled as he smiled. "If you decide to stick around for a few weeks, you should meet my wife, Jordan. She doesn't ride at your level, but horses and kids are kind of her passion."

"I'd love to." She swung her feet around to the floor as Dr. Sheehan made his way to the front door, the quick movement making her head swim again. She rested her forehead on her hand.

"I'll call tomorrow with the name of a doctor. In the meantime, take it easy."

"I will."

As the door closed behind the doctor, Devin appeared in the kitchen door with a glass of water. He crossed the room and handed it to her. "All good?"

"Yeah, he said I probably passed out because I was overwhelmed by the sight of the three fine-looking Cole brothers."

"Ha-ha, you're hilarious. What did he really say?"

Lacey took a deep breath. She'd wanted to gauge how things were with Devin before she had this conversation with him, but it looked like it wasn't going to happen on her timetable. "Can we take a walk? I've been sitting for days."

"Sure, if you feel up to it. I'd like to go out and see Reggie anyway." He held his hand out to her and, after a moment's hesitation, she slid her fingers into it, trying not to think about the way his skin warmed to hers and how right it seemed to link her hand with his.

He felt strong as he pulled her to her feet, and when she looked into his eyes, she realized how clear they were, how focused and steady. She hadn't seen him like that in a long time. It made her hopeful, a feeling she didn't have the luxury of allowing herself, not anymore. "There's something I want to talk to you about."

"Me, too." He opened the door for her, and she walked through it, taking a deep breath of the fresh country air.

Devin put his free hand in the small of her back, and she shifted away from him. They walked in silence for a few seconds as she looked around the property. "It's really beautiful here with the pastures and the fields. It's not exactly what I expected, but I like it."

"Yeah. The place looked pretty run-down when I got home a couple of months ago. Apparently, there have been some cash flow problems. Tanner's doing everything he can to shift gears and make it profitable again. It's just taking some time."

"He didn't tell you?"

"Maybe, or maybe I just didn't listen. I'm not sure which. Not sure it matters, really. It's easy for me to say now that I'd have come if I'd known, but the truth is, I probably wouldn't have."

"You should cut yourself a little slack, Devin. You love your brother. You love this ranch. That hasn't changed."

"Not as much as I should have. I'm not selling myself short, but I have to be honest with myself. It's one of the pillars of recovery. *Hi, my name's Devin and I'm an addict.*"

Hearing him say it so matter-of-factly was shocking. She'd known that he had the tendency to indulge a little too much and party a little too hard, but she hadn't realized how bad it had gotten until she'd seen the difference in him today.

He stopped by the fence to the pasture and whistled. Reggie lifted his head from the grass but he didn't move. Devin leaned his cane on the wood rail, dug a couple of carrot pieces out of his pocket and held them out. Reggie's nostrils flared and he took a few hesitant steps toward Devin and stalled, giving his owner the side-eye.

Lacey smothered a smile. Devin's horse seemed almost as mad at him as she was. She clicked her tongue. "C'mere, Reggie."

The big horse ambled to the fence and nudged Lacey's hand so she would scratch behind his ears. She obliged, murmuring to him that he was a good boy.

After getting his scratch from Lacey, Reggie gently nuzzled the carrot pieces from Devin's hand before shoving his nose into Devin's hair.

Devin laughed, his eyes lighting as he ran a hand down Reggie's neck. "I missed you, you crazy horse."

Lacey looked away. She wanted to remember the Devin who left her alone in a hotel room in Vegas. To remember the anger that fueled her as she drove from Oklahoma to Alabama. She couldn't afford to get distracted.

She came here to get him to sign divorce papers. And that was exactly what she was going to do.

Devin glanced at Lacey, who was leaning on the fence, her chin on her arms.

"I'm so sorry, Lacey." The words were out before Devin knew he was going to say them.

Her eyebrows shot to her hairline. "For what, exactly?"

"There are so many things to apologize for, I'm not sure where to start. But I think I should start with not taking responsibility that morning in Vegas. And not having enough guts to apologize face-to-face and depending on my horse to get the job done."

"Is that what leaving Reggie with me was about? An apology?"

"It seemed like a good idea at the time." His face went warm and he turned his head away from her too-knowing eyes, focusing on some trees in the distance. The tops were blowing in the late-afternoon breeze, the leaves flipping to reveal the silver underside.

A storm was coming, which seemed a fitting metaphor for the changes raining down on him if Lacey's babies were his. "I didn't know what to say to you. That morning, all I could think was that I'd finally done it. I'd done the thing that would finally drive you away, too."

"You mean, telling me you'd loved me for years and you wanted to marry me, so much that you couldn't wait another day?" There was an edge of bitterness to her tone, and he didn't blame her.

Because he felt like a total jerk, he pulled his ninety-day chip from the pocket of his jeans and held it in his fist, so he could remember that who he was now was not who he was then. He was a person who owned up to his responsibility. He was a person who found his strength in a higher power.

He was a person who told the truth, no matter how hard it was. "I was high that whole weekend. I don't have any memory of getting married. I don't remember anything about the weekend until I woke up in the bed and you were there."

Angry tears glittered on the edge of her lashes. "It was all a lie?"

He let out a frustrated sigh. "That morning—I was ashamed, knowing I'd done something so huge and couldn't remember. I let you down. There's nothing I can say to make that better."

When she looked back at him, her dark eyes were inscrutable. "I want a divorce. I mean it, Devin."

He let the words hang in the air for a minute. They shouldn't hurt, but somehow that didn't stop the sting. "I'd do just about anything for you, Lace, but I need some time to think about it."

"Why?" He could hear the exasperation in her voice as she paced away from him down the fence line. "You said yourself you don't even remember getting married. You sure don't remember why."

Devin had hoped she would tell him about her pregnancy, tell him about the babies, but since she didn't, he would have to press the point. It was too important not to. "I have two very good reasons to take my time making a decision about it."

She whirled around. "What do you mean?"

His fist was clenched so tightly around his NA coin, he could feel it slicing into his skin. "I saw the ultrasound photo. I know about the babies."

"I see." Anger sparked in Lacey's eyes. "So, what, you think that gives you the right to dictate what I do?"

He walked closer to her and reached for her hand. She snatched it back. He sighed. "I think we don't have to figure everything out today."

She visibly took a deep breath. "I came here to tell you about them. To tell you that I'm prepared to raise them on my own. You made it pretty clear when you disappeared that you weren't interested in a long-term relationship."

One of the tenets of recovery was that you didn't make any huge life changes in the first year. In the space of one afternoon, he'd blown that to smithereens. "Give me a chance, Lace, please?"

Lacey rubbed her forehead. "Look, when I get checked into a hotel, I'll text you my contact info and maybe we can talk tomorrow."

"The nearest hotel is forty minutes away." Devin paused. "But we have plenty of room, if you want to stay. Tanner and I sleep upstairs. You can have the master bedroom downstairs."

Lacey hesitated, hanging back as Devin started for the house. When he turned back to look for her, she sighed. "Fine. I'll stay, but just until we get things figured out."

He grinned and she held up a hand. "To be clear, my staying doesn't change things. I'm still mad and I still want a divorce."

At least she was talking to him, so that was something, right? Devin spread his free hand wide. "I hear you."

He hadn't let himself think about what it meant yet, that they had babies on the way, and he knew they had a lot of talking to do. But he wasn't walking away. He'd done that and it hadn't gone so well.

This time, he was sticking around, no matter what that meant.

Chapter Three

Devin disappeared after he showed Lacey to her room, leaving her to look around the tidy space. She'd stuck to her guns with Devin but she wished she felt steadier, more sure she was doing the right thing.

When she'd been driving out here, she'd been fueled by so much anger that she didn't have space for questions. Now she'd seen Devin. All the feelings she'd had for him were trying to crowd out the anger, and she couldn't have that. Anger could be the only thing that was keeping her from falling apart.

She needed to remember he'd left her.

Maybe he'd gone to rehab, but he'd been out for months and hadn't bothered to get in touch with her. Not even a text.

She didn't want to think about the fact

that he hadn't been himself, that he'd been freaked out and scared. She didn't want to think about the friendly room he'd put her in, with the large windows and painstakingly hand-stitched quilt on the bed.

She picked up one of the family photos that lined the dresser, her hand inadvertently going to her stomach. She definitely didn't want to think about her babies and wonder if one of them would grow into a little boy with a head full of sun-kissed curls.

This situation was such a mess. She'd been so angry—was still so angry—but cutting Devin out of her life wasn't going to be as simple as a signature on some papers.

She'd known it the moment she'd seen him.

With a big sigh, she opened the door to the hall. It was still early evening but maybe she could make her excuses and just go to bed. She followed the scent of something incredible into the kitchen. She stopped short when she realized that it was Devin's brother Tanner alone, flipping burgers on the stove.

He looked up, not really with a smile, more just a deepening of the lines around his mouth. "Hi there. You hungry?"

"Yes, actually." She hadn't realized it until

she'd smelled the food cooking but she was starving. "Really hungry."

She looked around the room. Like the rest of the house, it had a fresh coat of paint, the cabinets a glossy bright white. A wire basket of multicolored chicken eggs sat in the center of a round oak table.

Tanner slid a burger onto a plate and piled caramelized onions on top of it. "There are some freshly washed greens in the fridge if you want a salad. We're trying to do better with the vegetables, now that we're growing them."

She found the colander of lettuce in the fridge and added some to her plate. "We're not waiting on the others?"

"Devin will eat when he gets back. Garrett lives in town and he went home."

Lacey sat down as Tanner slid a glass of tea in front of her.

"It's decaf, in case you're wondering."

"That's fine, thanks." As he joined her at the table, she tried to figure out a diplomatic way of asking where Devin was. As the silence stretched, she gave up and went for simplicity. "So, where's Devin?"

"He's at a meeting. Sticking to a routine is really important for him right now."

She put her fork down on the table. "The doctor told me to take it easy for a few weeks before driving back, but if you think my being here is going to jeopardize Devin's recovery, I can move to a hotel room tomorrow."

Tanner glanced up from his plate. "You're welcome to stay as long as you like. You're family."

Tears pricked in her eyes, and she blinked them away, horrified. More took their place until she was sniffling and swiping at her eyes. "This is so embarrassing. I'm sorry."

Tanner wordlessly stood, walked to the counter, picked up a napkin and handed it to her, his eyes kind. "Take a bite of your burger. I bet you'll feel better after you eat."

"Thanks." She sniffed again but took a bite, followed by another and another. And he was right. She did feel a little better. She licked her fingers before she remembered the napkin. "This is so good."

"Raised right here," he said, then winced. "It's been a while since we had mixed company. Probably shouldn't have mentioned that at the dinner table."

Lacey let out a genuinely surprised bark of laughter. "I was raised on a ranch, too. Trust me when I say I'm not squeamish. And this is delicious."

He almost smiled, and she felt an absurd sense of accomplishment. "We've made a shift from raising cattle the traditional way to grass-fed beef and free-range chickens. Organic vegetables. Got a ways to go to make a profit."

He was a man of few words—until you got him going on a topic that interested him. She tucked that away to remember about her new brother-in-law. "You're trying for a specific clientele."

He nodded, his mouth full.

Devin had said that Tanner was changing gears. It made sense in a market where farm-to-table was the hottest thing going. "Very smart. I'd love to see the whole operation tomorrow."

Tanner nodded. "I'll get Devin to show you around." He paused again and she realized that it was a habit of his, thinking before he spoke. "He's trying really hard, Lacey. I had my doubts, but that weekend in Vegas changed everything for Devin."

Suddenly, she lost her appetite. She put the burger down.

That weekend in Vegas had changed her

life, too. Permanently, irrevocably changed her life. She'd tried living in the moment for one crazy, romantic weekend.

And she'd changed her future forever.

The sun was just coming up the next morning when Devin heard Lacey come into the kitchen. Without looking, he pulled a second mug down from the cabinet and filled it with coffee for her, but when he turned around, he hesitated. "Can you... I mean, is it okay for you to have coffee?"

"Yep, I'm allowed one cup, which is good for everyone's health and well-being." She was dressed in jeans and boots and a loose T-shirt, her long dark hair in a ponytail. He tried to get a surreptitious glance at her stomach to see if there was any evidence at all of the babies growing there, but if there was, he couldn't see it.

She blew on the surface of the coffee and took a small test sip, her eyes closing as she swallowed.

He wasn't sure what to say to her or how to interact with her while sober and after...all that had happened between them. Which was one of the reasons he'd stayed away. How did you have a normal conversation with someone after... There was a reason that kind of stuff was saved for marriage. Of course, they *were* actually married, an event that Devin wished with all his heart that he could remember.

Bringing the mug to his lips, he washed down the last of his sausage biscuit. "Tanner's already out in the field, but he said you wanted a tour of the farm?"

She nodded with just a flicker of a smile, but he was taken back. A flash of a memory, of Lacey smiling up at him, secret laughter in her eyes. Now, at best, those eyes were wary.

"Grab a biscuit. Reggie's the only horse here now, otherwise, we could ride, but you can see a lot walking." He finished his coffee and swiveled to put his mug in the dishwasher before picking up his cane.

Lacey looked at the biscuits loaded with sausage and turned a shade of green Devin wasn't sure he'd seen before.

"Ah... Maybe wait on the biscuit. I'll make some plain ones tomorrow."

"You made those?"

"I did. I had to pick up some skills to make myself useful around here. Not much call for washed-up bronc riders." The words were getting easier, but letting go of the dream was still hard. He'd wanted to rodeo as long as he could remember. "I can make you something else?"

"Coffee's fine for now. And I'd love to see the farm." She stepped through the door, coffee in hand.

Devin pulled the front door shut behind them and stepped out into early-morning not-yet-stifling humidity. The birds were singing and he could hear the cows shuffling in the pasture. It was his favorite time of day.

"Are you okay to walk all over the farm?"

He shot her a grin. "Thanks for asking, but yeah, I make do."

She hesitated. Then asked, "What happened to you, Devin? You were favoring the good ankle, but you were competing. You were walking without a cane."

He went a few paces without speaking. There wasn't a simple answer. "It might be easier if I start at the beginning."

They ambled together down the dirt road toward the back of the property, one of Tanner's dogs, a Rottweiler-shepherd mix named Sadie keeping pace beside them. "I'm not blaming anyone, okay? Because I take responsibility for all the stuff I did. But, if you want to know how it started, I came off a horse training in Colorado and landed funny on my shoulder."

She narrowed her eyes. "I vaguely remember that."

"It wasn't dislocated, but I think maybe I strained a ligament or something. I went to the medical room to have it checked out and they gave me some painkillers so I could ride that night."

"For a strained shoulder?" She looked a little dubious.

"Yeah. I'm not saying they did the wrong thing, but the next time I had a little injury, I went back. More painkillers. And before I knew it, I needed pills to get through the day. I started riding broncs, instead of sticking to cutting, which I knew. And every day I got a little more reckless with my safety. Every day, I'd get a little more hurt. And the whole thing was a giant messed-up circle."

Lacey walked in silence beside him for a few feet until they broke through the trees. In front of them was a field of sunflowers. Their happy yellow faces were turned toward the east, where the sun was just breaking over the trees.

She caught her breath. "Oh, this is gorgeous."

"We'll cut these starting tomorrow. We sell

them to people who sell flowers at area farmers markets." He pointed through the trees. "Back that way, in the woods, Tanner's got some pigs. Not many right now because we're just learning, but the sausage in our biscuits this morning… Uh, never mind."

She looked away, but there was a curve to her lips when she looked back. "It sounds like you guys have a plan."

"Yeah. It's slow, but as word gets out, a few people are starting to place orders and stuff."

They walked another trail and came out on the far side of the pond. It was visible from the house but just a hint of a gleam in the distance. Years ago, his mother had put two Adirondack chairs in a clearing under a big oak tree. He'd painted them a bright cheerful yellow to match the swing on the front porch the first week he'd been home.

"Want to sit for a few minutes?" When Lacey nodded, he dropped into one of the chairs, stretching his leg out in front of him, resting his hand on the head of the dog, who settled beside him.

Lacey sat quietly in the chair next to him. He pointed up in the tree. "See that scraggly end of a rope tied around that branch up there? Garrett and I used to swing out over the pond and drop. Tanner, too, but he was older. My mom would sit here. She'd always squeal when the cold water splashed her."

A smile tugged at his lips. Thoughts of his mom were always a little bittersweet. Even all these years later he missed her.

"I bet you found lots of ways to make the water splash her."

Lacey's voice broke into his thoughts and he glanced at her, forcing the easy smile. "How'd you guess? Garrett would never splash Mom on purpose. He was always the people pleaser. Middle-child thing, maybe."

"And you were the baby, the boundary pusher."

Black sheep. That's how he always thought of himself. The troublemaker of the family, the one who didn't quite fit. "Yeah, not much has changed, I guess."

"I knew you were partying and I knew you were taking crazy risks, but I didn't know why. Devin, why didn't you ask someone for help? Why didn't you ask me?"

He'd wondered when she would circle back to that. He looked out over the pond, sparkling in the morning light, and let the peace seep into him. God knew he needed it. "I didn't want you to know how bad things had gotten. I didn't want anyone to know, but especially you."

He blew out a frustrated breath, lifting one shoulder and letting it drop. "You can see how well that turned out. But I also didn't want to quit competing, and the drugs dulled the pain."

When he glanced back at her, her brown eyes were wide and serious. "So that's why you use a cane now. Because you're in pain all the time and now there are no drugs?"

"I kept riding broncs with an ankle that was held together with pins and screws and luck. So yeah, that's why I need a cane." He stood and helped Lacey to her feet, holding her hand just a second too long, wishing for something he couldn't even name. "Come on, we've got more to see."

He led her down the trail that wound around the pond and to the backside of the cow pasture. The cows followed them along the fence, pets as much as they were product. But that was kind of the point, according to Tanner. A low-stress environment was good for the animals.

She walked slowly beside him, matching her pace to his. "Cows are peaceful, I think, especially when they're just grazing in a field."

"I think so, too. I like hearing them." He glanced over at her, hardly believing that she was here beside him when he'd thought he might never see her again.

He opened the gate to the backyard. "I'll get in trouble if I don't do my chores, so I'm going to check the nesting boxes for eggs. You can wait on the porch or I'll meet you inside if you're ready for something to eat."

"Oh, that sounds like a good plan. I'll see you inside."

Devin opened the back of the chicken coop and removed over a dozen eggs, but his mind was in the house, where Lacey was waiting. They'd talked about a lot of things this morning, but the one topic they'd studiously avoided was what happened next.

It was tempting to continue avoiding it, to hang on to that small bit of peace they'd managed to scrape together this morning, but he didn't choose comfort over the more difficult option anymore. He couldn't run from hard things.

Back in the kitchen, he waited until the eggs were safely put away before washing his hands and sitting down beside her. "You like the farm?"

"Love it. Tanner's done such a careful job planning. It's amazing."

"Good. I have a proposition for you."

She went still. "Am I going to like this proposition?"

"Probably…not. But in the end, you get what you want."

"Okay," she said slowly. "Tell me what you have in mind."

"I'll sign the divorce papers on one condition."

Lacey closed her eyes. When she opened them, the wariness that had disappeared during their walk this morning was back. For a little while, it had almost been like old times. And he was holding out hope that she'd felt it, too.

"What's the condition?"

He took a deep breath. "You stay here at the ranch until the babies are born. We'll still have to work out custody and all that, but after they're born, if you still want me to, I'll sign the papers."

"Devin, I have a life—a family—in Oklahoma. I'm staying for a few weeks if the OB says I need to, but I have to go home." She placed both hands on the table and pushed to her feet. "It's a crazy idea."

"It probably is, but that's the deal." He was so nervous, but he forced himself to keep a relaxed position in the chair.

"You know I could take you to court anyway."

"I know, but I'm really hoping you won't. Give me a chance to show you that I can be a better person. That I can be a man who'll show up for his family. If you don't stay, you'll never know."

There were twin spots of color high on her cheekbones. "I need some time to think about this, Devin."

"You can have all the time you need." A fragment of a memory flashed in his mind, the two of them outside a hotel room door, her hand on his cheek and love in her eyes. It took his breath away.

He prayed that once she gave it some thought, she would want to stay.

And he would have a second chance.

Chapter Four

Lacey was 100 percent sure she'd lost her mind. She'd spent the previous day, including the last eight hours when she should've been asleep, trying to decide if she should stay in Red Hill Springs.

She didn't even want to go into the kitchen for breakfast and she was *starving*. It would be a long six months if she spent the whole time avoiding Devin.

The reasons she'd come here for a divorce hadn't changed. Devin was a risk-taker, the life of the party, a crowd-thrilling rodeo standout. He said he'd changed, but desperation had gotten him to this point. What would happen to her when he wasn't desperate anymore?

He'd left her.

He'd lied to her.

Her hand spread across the barely visible rise in her abdomen where their babies were growing. She leaned her head against the door to the bedroom, praying for guidance, for wisdom…for backbone, even.

The back door slammed and she jumped away from the bedroom door, her heart pounding in her chest until she realized it was the guys going out to work. She cracked the door, slowly letting out a breath. Sadie lifted her head and gave a soft woof.

Otherwise, silence.

Feeling like she should be on tiptoe, she eased down the hall, through the living room and into the kitchen with Sadie shadowing her. Fluffy white biscuits were waiting for her on top of the stove and for a second she stared at them. Devin had remembered to make them plain. It was a small thing, but she tucked it away in her mind. She picked one up from the pan, slathered it with butter and took a big bite, her eyes nearly crossing. It was so good.

The back door banged open and she dropped her biscuit, which was quickly gobbled up by the dog.

"Well, hey." Devin, all six feet three inches of him, stepped into the kitchen.

She swallowed hard, wishing she'd started with coffee, or juice or something that would make her mouth just a little less dry. "Mmm."

"That good, huh?" His face split into a grin, and her pulse gave a traitorous leap.

"Delicious." She swallowed again. "What's up on the farm today?"

"Cutting sunflowers and loading them into buckets to sell at some of the farmers markets around here. Come on down later if you want. We can pull a chair up under a shade tree. Garrett will be around this afternoon to help, too." He lifted a large orange drink cooler off the counter. "Forgot the water. See you later?"

She nodded. "Sure."

Her eyes lingered on the door as it closed behind him. He looked good. He looked happy. Healthy.

She picked up another biscuit and dropped into a kitchen chair, giving the dog a warning look. "You're not getting this one, so you can stop it with the pitiful sad eyes."

It was a darn good biscuit, but suddenly she wasn't that hungry. The shock of their conversation yesterday afternoon still hadn't faded. Devin's story of how he got addicted to painkillers was so raw and real. And he'd been so good at hiding it that she'd witnessed it happening and hadn't even realized it.

How could that even happen? How had he gotten so low and she hadn't noticed? That was on her.

She sighed and got up to pour herself a glass of orange juice. Whether she was hungry or not, the babies needed calories and so did she if she didn't want a repeat of the fainting incident.

It didn't seem real that she was carrying twins. That she was a *mother* and in six months' time she'd be holding them in her arms. She couldn't afford to take chances. In the arena, sure, she'd pushed limits—hers and her horse's. But even then, the risks had been calculated.

Marrying Devin had been the biggest risk of her life. She'd been afraid she couldn't trust him, and guess what? She'd been right.

But he'd said he loved her. With tears in his eyes and the ring of truth in his voice, he'd said the words she'd wanted to hear.

And the truth—the real truth—the dirty little secret she'd been hiding, even from herself, was that she'd been in love with Devin for years. She'd fallen hard from the moment she'd met him. And that was the most dangerous secret of all. She wanted to stay here. She wanted to know Devin, the real Devin who didn't hide behind success, alcohol and that shiny gold rodeo buckle. She wanted to know if she'd fallen in love with the real Devin or if everything she'd thought about him was just an illusion.

The glass trembled in her hand. What was she thinking? She needed to hang on to her anger. She'd waited for him for over three months. She'd given him the power to hurt her… *And he had.*

She couldn't forget that. Falling in love with him again was not an option. Devin was all flash and glory. Babies were bottles and dirty diapers and not the fun kind of sleepless nights.

No. A marriage needed a stronger foundation than a drug-induced fantasy. In the daylight, she could see reality and reality said she couldn't trust him. Not yet. Maybe not ever. She had to protect herself.

Because, just like in an airplane cabin losing pressure, she had to put her oxygen mask on first so she could be there to protect her babies. And no matter what, they had to be her first priority.

So she would go to the sunflower field and she would build a friendship with Devin for her babies' sake. She would search for the answers to her questions about who Devin really was. But she absolutely would not, under any circumstances, fall in love with him again.

In the distance, Devin heard the dog's joyful bark and squinted toward the house. Lacey was walking down the dirt lane between pastures, throwing a ball for Sadie, who would chase it down, return it and bark her head off until Lacey threw the ball again. Lacey laughed, her head thrown back, long dark hair trailing in loose waves down her back.

And watching her, Devin could barely breathe. All morning long his mind had been on their conversation last night, wondering if she'd give him a chance. Wondering if she still had feelings for him at all and if she'd made a decision.

Sadie caught sight of him and streaked down the road, cutting across the field when she saw Tanner instead. "Ah. I see who's really loved here."

Lacey started across the field toward him,

her crisp citrus scent reaching him before she did, the sweet aroma mingling with the green scent of the sunflowers. He drew in a deep breath as she lingered beside him.

"What are you doing?"

"Getting these ready to be sold." He glanced up at her, but his hands kept moving, prepping the flowers for transport—sliding netting over the sunflower blossom and a wide straw over the stem. He placed the flower in a five-gallon bucket at his feet and glanced up at her. "Sunflowers seem like they would be hardy, but they break easily. Underneath they're a lot more fragile than people think."

"Huh." She raised her eyebrows and looked down at her hands, where thin silver and turquoise rings shimmered on her fingers.

He narrowed his eyes. "What's that supposed to mean?"

"Oh, nothing."

Devin leaned against the table where he was working and studied her. He was self-aware enough—now—to get what she was saying. But he didn't want to talk about how mushy he was on the inside or how brittle he was on the outside. "Well, if you're gonna stand here, the least you can do is help."

Lacey shot him a look but picked up a sunflower, slid a straw over the stem and handed it to him.

In turn, Devin pulled the protective netting over the bloom and stuck it in the bucket. He turned to her, holding his hand up for a high five.

When she gave it to him with only a slight eye roll, he grinned. Progress. They made a good team.

The thought came with a little pang. He and Lacey had been a team in lots of ways for a long time. He'd lost track of the appearances they'd made together promoting the rodeo. There'd been questions for years about whether they were a couple, and the two of them had always laughed it off.

"Best friends," they'd said. "We know way too much about each other for a relationship."

It seemed pretty ironic now that what stood between them was the terrible secret he'd been hiding and the wall Lacey had put up to protect herself. For all of their sakes, especially two little babies he had yet to meet, he prayed they could get beyond it.

Pushing the envelope had been his MO. He was always good for a gasp from the crowd. And he'd loved the approval and the admiration of an audience. But the proposition he'd made to Lacey seemed like the biggest risk he'd ever taken. He wasn't just risking his heart, he was risking the peace he'd found here. In a real way, risking his future.

It didn't make sense—not in a practical way—what he was asking, but when he thought about their babies, it made all the sense in the world. His security and peace were nothing compared with theirs.

His fingers brushed against Lacey's as he took the flower, and she jerked her hand back like she'd been burned.

He sighed as he slid the netting over the deep yellow bloom. "So have you had a chance to think about our conversation yesterday morning?"

She breathed, the words flowing out of her with her exhalation. "I haven't been able to think about anything else."

His fingers stilled for a moment, but then he took the next flower, torn between wanting to hear what she had to say and wanting to be able to imagine he had a chance with her.

He opened his mouth to ask, just as his brother Tanner strode out of the field of sunflowers with two five-gallon buckets of flowers, Sadie ambling along beside him. *Perfect* timing.

"Devin put you to work?" Tanner nodded to Lacey, who shot him a breezy smile.

"Got to earn my keep. These sunflowers are gorgeous."

Devin scowled as he tugged another net over the head of a sunflower. "We were right in the middle of something, Tanner."

Tanner took one look at Devin's face and a single quirk of a smile flitted across his face. He pulled one of the newly cut stems out of the bucket and handed it to Lacey. "For you. The only payment you're likely to get out of a day's work at Triple Creek Ranch."

"And well worth it."

Devin rolled his eyes. "If you two are done, can we please get back to work?"

Lacey shrugged at Tanner and turned back to the table, carefully sliding a straw over one of the stems they would be selling.

Tanner gestured at the buckets on the ground beside Lacey. "Make sure Devin's the one picking these up when it's time for the next batch of flowers. They're really heavy."

"I've got it, Tanner." Devin tried to keep the edge out of his voice.

With a shrug, Tanner lifted a trio of empty

buckets and disappeared between the rows of sunflowers.

"He seems sweet."

Devin sighed as he lifted the next bucket of flowers to the table.

"Why doesn't he have a wife and a couple of kids by now?"

The bucket slammed onto the table, water sloshing over the side. Devin steadied himself against the unexpected wave of grief.

Lacey looked up in alarm. "What's wrong? Did you hurt your ankle?"

He should be able to handle an innocent question by now. The accident was simply a part of his story, something that happened in the past. He just wasn't prepared for her to ask it. "Nothing's wrong. It's… Look, don't bring this up with Tanner, okay? He lost his wife and baby in the same accident that killed our parents."

Tears formed in her eyes. She looked away. "I'm sorry. I didn't know. I never should've made that kind of assumption."

"It's okay. It is. It just…creeps up on you from time to time. You think you've gotten used to the idea that it happened and you've moved on and then, well, you're not okay.

And that stinks. I don't think Tanner's been okay for a really long time."

"He must've been so devastated." She laid her hand over his and laced their fingers together. "You were both so young."

He turned toward her, bringing her hand to his chest. He didn't want to wait anymore. "What do you say, Lace? Are we going to give this thing a chance?"

She shook her head and his heart plummeted to his feet. "What we're doing seems so backward. You don't get married, pregnant and *then* decide whether or not to stay together. I mean, who does that?"

"Maybe we do." He tucked one long dark curl behind her ear. "I mean, so *what*? We're married. We're pregnant. The pressure's off. Now we have a real chance to see what it's like to be together. Without the press, without the cameras. Without all the other stuff. Just—us."

Her gaze locked on his. She whispered, "I feel like I barely know you."

"That's exactly why you should stay." Devin kissed her fingers, still laced with his. "Give us a chance, Lacey. That's all I'm asking for."

"I gave us a chance, Devin. And we both

saw how that turned out." She pulled her hand away. "But I'll stay. Because our babies need a dad. And because one way or another, I want to be free of this hold you have over me. I care about you but I'm not along for the roller coaster anymore. I've had enough adventure."

She backed away from the table. "I'll see you at dinner. I need some space right now."

Devin watched her walk away, a knot that felt like a boulder in the pit of his stomach. It was too much to expect her to trust him so soon after what he'd done. But she was staying and he had six months to prove to her that he was a different person. That he was a man who knew how to be responsible, who would step up when things got hard and take care of his family.

He had six months to win her heart.

Chapter Five

As Lacey finished her dinner that night, she noticed that conversation had suddenly stopped. She glanced up. Devin was staring at her intensely, one finger touching his nose. She looked at Garrett, who had his hand nonchalantly over his mouth, with one of his fingers touching *his* nose. Tanner, oblivious, was taking his last bite of the simple spaghetti casserole she'd put together when they came in from the sunflower field.

She glanced back at Devin and he pointedly tapped his nose. She hesitantly raised her finger to her nose. "Not…it?"

Tanner's head jerked up, his shoulders falling as he noted the position of each of their fingers. He pushed back from the table with his plate in his hand. "You guys are so immature. Lacey, I expected better from you."

She laughed. "Sorry, Tanner. I love cooking but I hate doing dishes."

"I have never once won 'not it,'" Tanner grumbled. "Not cool."

Deadpan, Garrett handed Tanner his plate. "Thanks, bro. You're the best."

Lacey covered the little bit that remained of the spaghetti casserole and started to clear the table for Tanner, who took the plates from her and shooed her from the room.

In the living room, Garrett fiddled around on the piano, playing an old Beatles song. She hummed along as she walked out the door onto the porch. Taking a deep breath of the clean country air, she leaned on the rail, letting the cool breeze ruffle her hair.

The song changed to a familiar James Taylor song, a cowboy lullaby she'd heard her dad play often over the years. She heard the murmur of voices, and a guitar joined the piano. Devin's pure, clear tenor rose with the melody. A lump formed in her throat.

She liked things in categories and when things were murky in her mind, she felt out of focus. Devin defied category. When she first met him, she'd thought he was sweet and fun, if a little reckless. Later, after they'd been friends for a while, she'd thought she had figured out all his layers.

She'd been wrong about that.

For the last few months, she'd thought he was a total jerk. She'd been wrong about that, too. But now? She had no idea what to think about this person. She didn't know him at all. And she didn't know if what she was seeing now was the real Devin or a new Devin.

She looked up, whispering a prayer for discernment to the stars in the dark night sky. The stakes were so high. She needed God to guide her—trying to figure it out on her own wasn't working.

Devin's voice startled her. She'd been so far away in her thoughts that she hadn't even realized the music had stopped. "That was my mother's favorite song when she was pregnant with me. She wanted to name me James, but my dad wouldn't let her. He said she'd be calling me Sweet Baby James until I was thirty and he wasn't having it."

"Your dad had a point." She turned toward Devin with a smile. His face was half in the shadows and it occurred to her that her understanding of him was so much like that, only half in the light. He'd talked about the farm.

His love for the land. He'd even told some stories about him and Garrett when they'd been little. But he'd never really talked about his mom and dad.

Now that they were facing the prospect of being a mom and dad, it was meaningful to her that Devin would share something about them. He'd been loved by his mom from before she even knew his face—that much was clear.

She hadn't had that same experience with her own mother. It had been just her and her dad since she was a little girl. She rubbed her belly idly. It didn't matter that she'd never seen the faces of her twins. She loved them already.

Devin held the guitar by the neck and leaned a hip on the porch railing, his eyes on hers. He swung it up, settled it under his arm and began to pick the tune of a familiar hymn.

She took a deep breath, letting her thoughts—and if she were honest, doubts—fly to the stars along with her prayers. "I learned how to play the recorder in the fifth grade."

"Oh yeah? Maybe we can start a band."

She snorted a laugh. "Now, that would be

something to tell our kids about. I never knew you played the guitar."

"I got my first guitar for my birthday when I was nine and taught myself how to play. I bought this one later. Garrett brought it over after I got out of rehab." He shrugged. "I think playing it now makes me feel more connected to who I was before."

"Before rehab?"

"No." He paused and glanced out to the pasture where his horse was nibbling on grass in the moonlight, his eyes narrowing against his memory. "Before the accident. I stopped playing after that. My mom was always singing along to something, but after she died, I don't know, it just didn't seem right to have music in the house." He looked at her then, his fingers stilling the vibration of the strings before he picked up the melody again. "Seems silly, saying it out loud now. My mom wouldn't have wanted that."

"You were so young. Maybe it was your way of acknowledging what a huge loss it was." The more she got to know the Cole brothers, the more she realized how much life had changed for all of them the day of the accident. Devin was the youngest and Lacey had to wonder if all the reckless adventures

Devin chased had been an attempt to keep from actually feeling the grief of losing his parents.

But he was playing the guitar again and he was talking.

He was trying.

She took a deep breath, feeling like she was standing at the edge of a diving board, her toes over the edge, her balance wobbling. "I'm going to the doctor in the morning. You can come…if you want."

He stopped playing. "You're serious?"

"You want to?"

A grin split his face. "Yes! Yes, I want to!"

"The appointment is tomorrow morning at ten."

"Ten. Got it." He glanced at his watch and started for the house. "I gotta get out of here or I'm gonna miss my meeting."

"I'll be here when you get back."

He paused with the door half-open, looked back and shot her a smile. "I'm really glad."

"Me, too." She said it without thinking, but it was true. And the thought scared her.

Because it meant she had something to lose.

Lacey had a death grip on Devin's hand as they walked into the obstetrician's office. He waited beside her, trying not to intervene as the receptionist tried to tell her that Dr. Lescale wasn't taking new patients and Lacey patiently corrected her. When Devin saw Lacey's fingers tremble as she finally picked up the pen to sign in, his hand landed at the small of her back and didn't move until she was seated in the comfiest chair in the room.

He took the chair next to Lacey, his knees sticking out at an awkward angle, his cane leaning against the table next to him. He felt conspicuous. And like a giant. Like a giant conspicuous guy who didn't belong here.

The urge to reach in his pocket for his NA chip was almost irresistible. It wasn't a talisman, he knew that, but it was an object that grounded him. He reminded himself he belonged here. He was Lacey's husband and the father of the babies she was carrying. Maybe their relationship hadn't happened in the conventional way, but it was a fact: they were married.

He took a deep breath and looked around the room. Really looked. He scratched his neck and caught the eye of a guy a few chairs down who was sitting next to an extremely pregnant woman who was periodically crying into a tissue. He looked away quickly.

"Are you nervous?" Lacey's voice interrupted his thoughts.

"Me?" He waved away the concern. "Not at all. You?"

Her brows drew together. "Not really. I guess I'll be glad to know everything's okay, though."

The door opened. "Lacey Cole?"

Lacey stood, and Devin grabbed his cane, halfway out of his chair before the nurse held up her hand. "She'll be right back. We're just getting some info right now."

Another woman in baby blue scrubs came out and called a name, and the crying lady left. Her partner took a deep breath and stabbed his fingers through his hair. Devin gave the guy what he hoped was an empathetic look.

"Pregnancy is nuts, you know?"

Devin looked around for someone—anyone—else. Was the guy talking to him or talking to himself? To be safe, Devin nodded slightly.

"That your wife?" The guy hooked a thumb toward the door to the back.

So he was definitely talking to Devin. "Oh…uh…yeah. You?"

"Yeah. We'd only been married a year

when we found out she was pregnant. Good-bye, honeymoon, am I right?"

Devin guessed that depended on your point of view but didn't say anything.

It didn't seem to matter. The man kept talking. "I mean, she's been literally crying for months. Sometimes I think I'm gonna need a life jacket in my own house. I don't even know what she's crying about. For real, I don't think she knows what she's crying about."

Devin closed his eyes and imagined that he was on a beach in Florida. Soft white sand, the warm sun and a cool breeze, the sound of the waves smoothing the shore.

No one oversharing.

"Right, man?"

Devin opened his eyes. "Oh, uh, sure."

The door opened and the nurse looked at the hot pink sticky note attached to her finger. "Devin Cole? We've got a room available for your wife."

Devin was hobbling across the room before the nurse finished her sentence. He couldn't get the image of that woman crying into a tissue out of his head. Was Lacey going to be like that? Had she just not hit that stage?

He'd never seen a pregnant woman cry

like that. Granted, he hadn't been around that many.

Or any.

Walking through the door to the back room felt kind of like stepping into Narnia. It was freezing back here for one thing. And it was definitely a foreign land.

The nurse stopped in front of a door, knocked slightly, then opened it without waiting. Lacey was sitting on the exam table in a paper gown, fingers gripping the edge and bare feet dangling. Her eyes were wide and shiny. A sheet covered her upper legs.

She shrugged, with a sheepish sort of look on her face. "Here we are."

"Yep. Here we are." Hot prickles formed on the back of Devin's neck, beads of sweat forming on his forehead. He was not supposed to be here. Mortals were not supposed to be in Narnia.

"You look a little grim," Lacey said.

"No, it's fine. This is great. Really."

Lacey laughed. "Whatever you say."

He scrunched his nose at her.

The door flew wide. A petite woman wearing scrubs and a white coat strode in, stuck her hand under the sanitizer dispenser and turned to Lacey with a smile as she rubbed the gel on the surface of her hands. "I'm Dr. Lescale. Here's what I know—you're pregnant with twins, history of low blood pressure and fainting. And my friend Ash referred you to me."

"Right." Lacey held out a hand. "Lacey Cole. And this is Devin."

The sound of his name with hers never failed to jar him. He leaned back against the wall, taking the weight off his ankle and trying to be invisible.

The doctor looked at the computer monitor, scrolling and clicking. "Your vitals look good. Feeling okay?" At Lacey's nod, she picked up what looked like a remote control and raised the table while simultaneously sliding out a footrest for Lacey. "Let's see if we can hear those babies."

Devin shifted on his feet. He felt awkward but he knew it had to be nothing compared with how vulnerable Lacey was feeling. At least he had all his clothes on.

When Dr. Lescale had Lacey settled, she pulled out a little machine with a wand at the end of it. After squirting some gel onto the end of it, she ran it over Lacey's stomach.

"You're almost sixteen weeks along? You're going to be really showing soon."

Dr. Lescale looked up at Devin. "Come here, Dad."

With a gulp he hoped wasn't audible, he moved over to the doctor, who placed the wand in his hand and guided it into place.

The doctor narrowed her eyes, listening. "Just…there."

With that, a whooshing sound, almost like the sound of a washing machine, filled the room. A big smile spread across Lacey's face and her eyes filled.

Dr. Lescale smiled, too. "Good strong heartbeat for Baby A. Now let's find Baby B."

With a sure hand, the doctor guided the wand to just the right spot and the sound of another heartbeat filled the room.

Without warning, a tear spilled down Devin's cheek. He lifted his shoulder and rubbed it away. But as the sound continued, so did the tears, and the fact that he was going to be someone's daddy became not some nebulous fact that he knew, but a genuine reality, right there under his hand.

A tear splashed onto the paper cover of the exam table, and Dr. Lescale looked up with surprise. She immediately removed the wand and handed Lacey a tissue. "I'm just going to give you two a minute while I get some pre-natal vitamins together for Lacey."

The door closed behind the doctor and Devin remained where he was, his hands spread wide on the exam table, letting it take his weight, his head bowed. He took a shuddering breath, dragging air into his lungs.

The first touch of her hand was so soft he almost missed it. But again he felt it, the featherlight touch in his hair. He should open his eyes, say something funny, brush off the seriousness of the moment, but he couldn't do it.

He couldn't pretend that his tightly leashed control hadn't shattered the moment the first beat of his baby's heart sounded in the room. He couldn't pretend at all.

Slowly he raised his head. Her fingers were still in his hair. Her eyes on his. "Dev,'' she said hesitantly.

He forced a smile. "I'm okay. I'm fine. Sorry I got emotional."

"Don't do that."

"What?"

"Pull away from me. They're your babies, Devin. It's okay to be a little overwhelmed when you hear their hearts beating for the first time."

He swallowed hard and tried to smile again and make a joke, but the smile was a quirk of one corner of his mouth, the laugh a choking swallow.

Devin took a deep breath and straightened as the door to the hall opened and the doctor stuck her head in. Lacey's hand fell back to her side.

"I'll meet you at the car." Devin felt her sigh, but he couldn't stay in that tiny room with the walls closing in. And he couldn't put a name to the emotion, but it felt more threatening than the most dangerous bronc he'd ever faced in the arena.

Chapter Six

Lacey opened the passenger-side door and slid into the seat. Devin handed her a white paper bag that smelled suspiciously like french fries. She sent him a look out of the corner of her eye and opened the bag. Pulling out a few and shoving them in her mouth, she asked, "How did you know I was starving?"

"I'm the one who cooks breakfast, remember? I know you didn't eat." He handed her a milkshake. "I also seem to remember you once told me that fries without a milkshake are 'just another root vegetable.'"

"Oh, you are the best." She took the lid off the milkshake, grabbed another handful of fries and dipped them, closing her eyes as she savored her favorite post-rodeo indulgence.

"Whoever built a fast-food place next to an OB's office was a genius."

Devin put the truck in gear and drove toward the farm. She finished her fries in silence, brushed the salt from her fingers and crumpled up the bag. "So. Are we going to talk about what happened in there?"

He didn't take his eyes off the road. "Nope."

Lacey thought for a minute and then shrugged. "Okay."

He looked at her then—an incredulous, disbelieving look.

"I mean it, Devin. You can have your feelings without talking about them. I have feelings all the time that I keep to myself."

His eyebrows slammed together. "Like what?"

She sat back against the seat and looked out the window so he wouldn't see her smile. "Like I'm not going to tell you."

He sighed and stared out the windshield as he drove, both hands on the steering wheel. Three long minutes ticked by in silence before he said, "I was distracted when I came into the exam room, wondering when you were going to start with the nonstop crying, and then I heard the heartbeat and it was…" His voice choked again. "It was so real, you know? That there's a baby—our baby—two of them. It was a little overwhelming is all."

Lacey considered being smug that she'd gotten him to talk about his feelings, but what he'd said was so right on target that she just smiled.

He growled. "Happy?"

"Yeah." She laughed.

A few seconds later, she said quietly, "When I first found out I was pregnant, I was kind of mad about it, like, of *course* that would happen to me, but then I heard their heartbeats… And all of a sudden, I was their mother. And it didn't matter how it happened. They were mine." She glanced over at him. "It rocked my world."

He didn't say anything, didn't even take his eyes off the road, but he reached over and laced his fingers with hers.

She stared at their hands, wanting to deny that her stoic facade was cracking. She didn't *want* to feel anything for him. He'd broken her heart.

They'd spent so much time together in the past. Hours in barns at various arenas around the country. Hours on the road. She'd told him everything. And apparently he'd re-membered it, like he remembered that she only really liked french fries dipped in chocolate milkshake.

How could she not have noticed that in all the time they'd spent together, he'd told her almost nothing? She drew in a breath and bolstered her resolve. He'd skipped out when things had gotten serious in the exam room because that was what Devin did. And despite his tears, despite the fact that they were tied together by their babies, she wasn't going to fall for him. She couldn't... Because if she couldn't trust her own heart, what could she trust?

In her mind, she heard her daddy's voice and could almost feel his finger tapping her forehead. "You trust your head, punkin'. Not your heart. Your heart will go after that brass ring every time. Your head will tell you if you have what it takes to make it."

She had to trust her brain and approach her relationship with Devin the same way she would the barrels, with mental toughness. In the ring, if she let emotion—or nerves, or fear, or worry—ruin her concentration, she lost her edge. Her horse, Magpie, was sensitive to Lacey's tiniest change in attitude and she depended on Lacey to be relaxed and focused and confident.

She'd learned that lesson from the time she was old enough to get on a horse and trot around the practice ring. Mind over matter.

In the back of Lacey's mind, though, she knew that no matter how much her dad told her to use her brain, it wasn't intellect that kept her chasing cans. It was passion. And instinct…and heart.

The truck bounced over a rut. Devin winced. "Sorry."

When Lacey looked up, she realized she had no idea where they were. She'd been so deep in thought that she hadn't noticed Devin had passed Triple Creek Ranch.

"Where are we?"

"Red Hill Farm. There's an equine therapy program here. The lady who runs it has a horse she wants me to take a look at." He pulled to a stop by a huge white antebellum house. A handful of little children were playing in a fenced area in the backyard. A woman with one long red braid over her shoulder and a baby in a sling across her chest walked out of the barn.

She met them mid-driveway, one hand holding the baby in place, the other outstretched to shake Devin's hand. Her eyes widened as a particularly shrill shriek split the air. "Sorry about the noise. Preschool is out for the week, so they're all here."

"No worries." His hand on Lacey's back, Devin introduced her to Jordan Sheehan, whose face lit up.

"Lacey Jenkins. Wow, it's a pleasure. I've seen you ride—you're amazing."

"Thanks." Lacey smiled. "So let me see if I've got this right… You're married to the pediatrician and you have…a lot of kids."

Jordan looked confused for a moment before she cracked up laughing. "We have two kids. Levi—the one sliding like a maniac over there—is almost five. And this little peanut here is Essie. She's two months old. The rest of the kids are my sister's. She and her husband are foster parents."

"Oh, wow. I'm only having two and it seems overwhelming. I can't imagine."

"Congratulations!" Jordan grinned. "I get it. But trust me, you get used to the noise level."

Devin walked toward the covered arena where a beautiful red-and-white paint mare was circling. He rested his arms on the top of the fence. "So what's her story?"

Jordan sighed. "She's a one-owner horse. Sweet as buttercream frosting. Her elderly owner was put into a nursing home recently and the children thought it would be great to donate Dolly to our program."

"Seems reasonable."

"She's so gentle. We all thought she would be a good fit…until we got her near the kids. She's terrified of them."

Devin dug a sugar cube out of his pocket, stuck his fingers in his mouth and whistled. The mare's head came up and she trotted closer, drawn to the sugar. As she approached the fence, one of the kids on the playground yelled. Dolly wheeled immediately, speeding to the opposite end of the arena, ears pinned back.

"Yeah. That pretty much sums it up." The baby whimpered, and Jordan jiggled her.

"I hate that it's not going to work out for you to use her in therapy." Devin picked up his cane from where he'd leaned it against the fence. "Mind if I take a closer look, ride her a little bit?"

"Not at all. Let me just take the baby over to the nanny."

"I'll hold her," Lacey volunteered.

"If you're sure, that would be great. Mrs. Matthews has her hands full today." A few seconds later, Jordan placed her baby girl in

Lacey's arms. "Just yell if you need anything. Ready, Devin?"

With her heart in her throat, Lacey looked into the little-bitty face. Essie's skin was almost translucent, auburn lashes fanning out over her cheek. Her tiny little rosebud mouth worked in her sleep, as if she were dreaming of her next meal.

Lacey drew in a shaky breath and walked across the yard, easing into a swing under the wide branches of an oak tree. She thought she'd understood what it meant that she was about to have a baby—two babies—but holding this sweet girl made her realize… She had no idea what she was getting into.

Rocking gently, baby Essie tucked safely in her arms, she glanced at the gate as Devin rode out on Dolly. He took her into a simple figure eight, concentrating on the shape, letting her know he was leading. Every time she'd get a little distracted by the noise of the kids, he'd redirect her to the pattern they were walking.

He was so sensitive to every flick of the horse's ears, every twitch of her shoulder. And he calmed her effortlessly. Lacey had seen him do it a thousand times.

She admired him so much. She was also

confused by him, her emotions all over the place when it came to their relationship. And the little bundle in her arms reminded her just how high the stakes were.

Hours later, finally back at Triple Creek, Devin had Dolly firmly ensconced in a stall in the barn nearest the pasture where Reggie was spending his retirement. She'd be able to hear the other horse and smell him but not see him. He suspected that part of the problem with Dolly's behavior was that she'd been the only horse her owner had. She was spoiled… And she was sad.

He shook a few extra oats into her bucket and scratched her neck just under her mane. "There you go, sweet girl. I'll see you in the morning."

His body ached with exertion as he limped his way up the stairs and into the house. He hadn't ridden in a long while and his ankle was in revolt. Since he didn't take painkillers anymore, he was hoping a couple of acetaminophen and a hot bath would at least take the edge off.

He'd taken only a couple of steps into the room when he heard the yelling coming from behind a closed door. He stopped, staring at nothing while he sucked in a long breath… and opened the door to the office.

Tanner was standing over the desk, his hands braced on either side of some kind of ledger. Devin could only imagine that it was the ranch finances.

Garrett was sprawled in a leather chair, a bored expression on his face, as if he'd heard this lecture a thousand times before. And Devin was sure that he had, because without a doubt, the lecture was about Devin. He just wasn't sure exactly what he'd done to deserve it. This time.

Devin leaned against the door frame. "What is it, Tanner? Did I forget to unload the dishwasher? Miss an egg in the henhouse? Leave wet clothes in the dryer? What?"

Garrett sat up a little straighter, his voice a warning. "Dev…"

Devin stopped Garrett with a hand held up against the words. "No, Garrett. I've never in my life been able to do anything good enough for Tanner."

Garrett stood up, putting himself between the two brothers, oldest and youngest. "That's not exactly fair, Dev."

Devin was tired, in pain and just so over

the chip on his brother's shoulder. "What did I do wrong this time, Tanner?"

"The horse."

At the words, Devin advanced. "Since when do I need permission to bring a horse home? It's a ranch, still. Right?"

Tanner's eyes were emotionless. "Since we don't have the money to feed it."

Devin recoiled, his mind struggling to make sense of what Tanner said. "What?"

Tanner closed his eyes and stretched his neck, rubbing the side of it with his hand. When he opened his eyes, he said, "We're barely staying afloat."

A coughing noise interrupted them. The three of them turned in tandem to find Lacey standing in the door. She tried a hesitant smile. "Dinner's ready?"

Tanner stalked toward the kitchen. "There's no sense in talking about this anyway."

Devin looked at Garrett, who shrugged.

When they were all seated around the table and grace had been said, Devin cut into his baked chicken. Without lifting his eyes, he said, "So let's talk about what we can do to make some money."

Tanner slammed his fork down and put his hands on the edge of the table, ready to push himself back. "This is not the time to discuss this."

Garrett put his hand on Tanner's shoulder. "Devin's right. You've been carrying this a long time. The ranch belongs to all of us. All of us need to figure out how to fix it."

"I can go into the other room so you guys can work this out." Lacey stood, but Tanner waved her back into her seat.

"You want to talk… Let's talk. I've done everything I can do to get this place back on its feet. And it's working. It's just not working fast enough."

"What's the bottom line, Tanner?" Garrett took a bite of his chicken and stabbed a piece of their homegrown asparagus.

Tanner's cheeks were ruddy. "When we inherited the farm, there was already substantial debt. I've paid it down but we're just not bringing in enough yet to get it paid off in time. We're gaining ground but…"

"…we need to brainstorm ideas for bringing in more cash." Devin picked up his sweet tea. "So who has ideas?"

Garrett raised his hand. "How about goats? You can drink the milk and make cheese and soap to sell."

Tanner got up and scrounged in the drawer

under the microwave, coming up with a half-used pad and a pen. He sat down and scribbled a word. "Okay, goats. Anything else?"

Devin gave Garrett a skeptical look. "I mean, don't get me wrong, I love goats, but we don't know how to make goat cheese or soap. What about bees? We could sell the honey at farmers markets, like we do the sunflowers."

Tanner wrote it down, but this time he made a face. "I think that's a great idea, but doesn't it take time for bees to make honey? We don't have a lot of time."

"True. Maybe we could rent space to a beekeeper. That would bring in a little money and bees are good on the farm, anyway." Devin looked down at the table. Garrett looked out the window, Tanner at the pad in front of him.

Lacey drew in a breath and all three of them focused on her. She glanced from one to the other. "No, I mean, I was just taking a breath."

"Oh." Devin slumped to the side.

"But…"

Tanner looked up at Lacey. "It couldn't be worse than goats or bees. No offense," he said to his brothers.

Garrett shrugged. "None taken."

"What's your idea, Lacey?" Devin was exhausted. His ankle ached and tension knotted his shoulders. He was ticked that Tanner hadn't told him and Garrett how bad things were. But they were in this together. All of them.

Lacey winced. "It seems silly... But in Oklahoma, a lot of farmers have roadside stands. Tanner has already been working at growing organic vegetables. We have zucchini out the ears. I saw the blueberry bushes in the field behind the pond and they're about to be ripe. We have eggs for days. Maybe we could...build a farm stand?"

Devin looked at Garrett and Tanner. He wasn't sure what the two of them were thinking but he was pretty sure his wife was brilliant.

Tanner wrote it down on the pad and then looked up. "We'll have to get a permit. But I have wood in the barn and, you're right, we have more vegetables than we know what to do with. I think it's a viable plan provided we think it through."

"Yes! Up top." Devin held up a hand for a high five.

Her gaze softened on his. "I'm already there."

Devin's grin slowly faded. He'd said that

to her once at a competition after a ride. She'd held up a hand for a high five and he'd pointed to the leader board and sent her a cocky smile. *I'm already there.*

He'd missed her. It just hit him how badly he'd missed his friend. She'd been there beside him, willing to stay, and he'd locked her out.

He didn't want to lock her out anymore.

Tanner cleared his throat, and Lacey looked away. His brother tapped the pad with his pen. "So I've got some researching to do."

Devin looked at his watch. "I've got to get to a meeting."

"Guess that means I've got the dishes." Garrett pushed back from the table.

Devin grabbed his cane. Lacey followed him through the living room to the front door and he turned back to her. "You're brilliant. In the morning, let's sit down and make sure we're tracking together. Okay?"

She nodded, and he wanted so badly to just drop a kiss on her lips, the way a husband would. But he knew she wasn't ready. They weren't ready.

Instead he smiled. "It's a date, then."

He'd seen his mom walk his dad to that same door a million times. He'd never realized that he wanted that. The admiration of the crowd was something. He'd never forget what it felt like to have them chanting his name.

But he would trade it all for the admiration of one woman. And he prayed that he could be the kind of man she could trust.

The kind of man she could love.

Chapter Seven

With country music playing softly in the background, Lacey hummed to herself as she rinsed her mixing bowls and spoons in the sink. Her fourth batch of zucchini brownies was in the oven. The first three batches had been, in order, too crumbly, too gooey, too zucchini-y. Way too zucchini-y. Even though that wasn't really a word.

Her goal was to perfect a few simple recipes so they could sell baked goods made with their own produce at the farm stand. So far, she hadn't been successful. But she wasn't a quitter. The guys might be quitting her brownies, though, if she couldn't come up with a decent recipe.

Baking gave her time to think, and even with the sound of the guys' hammers competing with her music, the farm was peaceful. It was strange, really. She'd always thought that racing barrels was the height of happiness for her. And maybe it *was* the ultimate in happiness, but she hadn't been content—not when she was always chasing the *next* win.

She loved the feeling of the wind in her hair, the exhilaration of the competition and the thrill of winning. She loved the competition and pushing herself, but contentment? Contentment was what she felt being a part of life on the ranch, working with Devin and Garrett and Tanner to make plans and create something new.

The timer beeped, and Lacey pulled open the oven to check on the zucchini brownies. They were slightly underbaked but she was hoping that they would be just the right amount of chewy when they cooled.

She heard the front door open as she slid the pan onto the top of the stove. With her quilted oven mitts still on her hands, she walked into the living room just as Devin placed a laundry basket full of clothes on the coffee table. "What's this?"

"Jordan brought over some maternity clothes."

"Aw, that's sweet. And the flowers?"

"They just reminded me of you." The last few weeks had blown by in a blur of discarded farm stand designs, permit paperwork and paint chips. And Devin had taken to picking whatever wildflowers were blooming and putting them in a blue-and-white splatterware pitcher in the kitchen—just because she liked them.

Last night he'd made lasagna from scratch because it was her favorite. He'd underestimated how long it would take to make by about two hours and his brothers had been ruthless, but she thought it was sweet.

"These are so pretty." Lacey added the flowers to the ones already on the table and turned around to see Devin leaning over the pan of brownies. She smacked him with the rooster side of the oven mitt. "I can't believe you! Sneaking a brownie when my back was turned."

He pointed to his mouth and let his eyes roll back in his head, and as much as she tried to act annoyed with him, she couldn't do it. "Good? Really good?"

"So good. What did you do?"

"The Triple Creek Ranch Triple Chocolate Brownie recipe is top secret." She pretended to lock her lips and throw the key out the window.

He very slowly put his fork down, and she felt the giggle rise in her chest. She took a step back, putting one oven-mitted hand up between them. "Uh-uh. Don't start with me, Devin. Go hammer something."

Devin advanced slowly, his eyes on hers. She turned to run, the laugh breaking free as he grabbed the oven mitt, tugging her back to him.

She laughed. "You have chocolate on your chin."

When she wiped it with a quick scrub of the hot pad, his smile faded. "You're so beautiful."

With his arms wrapped around her, she went still. She'd been very careful about touching him. But now, in his arms, she let herself imagine just for a minute that their wedding had been planned, their marriage for real…their love the forever kind.

She could paint a fantasy of herself right here in the kitchen, laughing at something Devin said, their babies in high chairs at the kitchen table. And it felt right.

"Lace…" His voice was husky in her ear.

She looked up and found his dark brown eyes intent on hers, and so close. When he leaned forward, she moved closer. She knew he was going to kiss her, and she wanted him to.

It was *so* tempting to let all her worries about the future go and just ride with the feeling, but she couldn't.

She wanted to cry at the injustice of it, but pretending things were different wasn't fair—to either of them.

With her hand still in the oven mitt on his chest, she said, "Wait, Devin."

He immediately let her go and stepped back, the realization of what almost happened all over his face. "I'm sorry. I didn't mean to assume anything…"

"No, it's not that, it's…oh." She blinked. "Hold on a sec."

"You okay?" His voice was concerned and he reached for her, his hand hovering somewhere around her elbow.

"Yeah, I'm fine." She laughed, slid the oven mitts off and took his hand. She placed it on the swell of her stomach. "There. Wait, no. *There*."

Lacey rested her hand over his and watched his face, waiting for him to realize what he was feeling. Wonder spread across his face as he let out an awestruck sigh. "He's kicking?"

She nodded. "I wasn't sure at first, but yeah. He—or she—is *definitely* kicking. I think maybe all the chocolate experiments I've been eating woke them up."

"It's our babies." His voice hitched on the words, and her heart ached. He cupped her face with both his hands and let his forehead gently touch hers. "I know our relationship is anything but normal, but the babies—I'm just blown away, Lacey."

And he was right. They were in a mess and everything was wrong. Everything was wrong except for the amazing rightness of their twins.

This time when he tilted her chin up, she didn't resist. When he brushed his lips across hers, she closed her eyes and leaned in, letting all her thoughts drift away and the feelings wash over her.

Until he lifted his head and gazed into her eyes with a soft, indulgent look and she froze.

He didn't say anything, just stood there with his heart in his eyes.

"I'm sorry, Devin." She took a step back, wishing they were still friends so she could give him a hug and tell him everything would be okay. But she didn't know that. What she did know was that they'd been down this road before. The only thing that was different was there was more on the line.

She took another step back, her chest tight. "I'm so sorry, but we can't do this, Devin. *I* can't do this."

"I know. Really, it's fine." He dropped his hands. His phone rang. He pulled it out of his pocket and looked at the readout. "I'll get this outside."

He was back a minute later, his hand over the receiver, his face gray tinged under his tan. "It's the mayor's assistant. The marshal of the Fourth of July parade got the stomach flu and they'd love 'a couple of former rodeo stars' to fill in."

"We can't do that," she whispered.

"I don't know how to get out of it. It's this afternoon." Even his whisper was miserable.

She rubbed her temples, wishing she could rub away the headache forming behind her eyes. She shrugged. "I mean…okay, sure. Whatever."

His eyes on hers, he took his hand off the mouthpiece and put the phone back to his ear. "Okay, yeah, we can do that." To Lacey, he mouthed, "I'm sorry."

Lacey sighed, every fiber of her being rebelling against acting the happy couple. She tossed the oven mitts onto the counter. "Yeah. Me, too."

* * *

Staging took place on the circular drive of the Red Hill Springs Middle School. Devin and Lacey were assigned the back of a candy-apple-red 1988 Corvette convertible that spent most of each year in Harvey Haney's barn. Someone had glitter-glued Marshal onto poster board and stuck it to each side of the car.

Lacey, in bright red boots, jeans and a cowboy hat, looked the part of a Memorial Day parade marshal. She was all smiles as one of the members of the marching band stuck his trumpet under his arm to help her into the back of the car. Her nearly waist-length hair bounced in loopy curls that made Devin's fingers itch to touch it.

The chaos on the middle school lawn was barely leashed, not even close to being controlled, when a woman in jeans and a navy blazer stopped next to him. "Devin Cole? I'm Wynn Grant… Mayor Grant. Thanks so much for filling in at the last minute. When I heard from Garrett that you and Lacey were in town, I just knew you'd be perfect to fill in."

"Glad I know who to blame. Nice to meet you." Familiar reflexes kicked in and he flashed a grin, tipping his hat forward over his eyes. Behind him, he heard Lacey smother a laugh with a cough. "Have you met Lacey yet?"

Wynn Grant turned to Lacey with a smile. "Thank you so much for letting us talk you into this. You're a champ."

"So, are there any instructions?" Devin asked.

"Just smile and wave. If you want to throw candy, there are a couple of buckets of fireballs on the seat."

"Yes, ma'am." About that time, Devin heard three sharp whistles. The marching band began to play and the volunteer firefighters started up the sirens.

The mayor was gesticulating and her lips were moving but he had no idea what she was saying. Finally, a pickup truck pulled up beside her with a similarly glittered sign that said Mayor stuck to the side doors and at least a dozen kids in the truck bed.

Mayor Grant said goodbye, or at least Devin assumed that was what she said, and Devin climbed into the back of the red Corvette beside Lacey. Mr. Haney, in his ever-present overalls, slid into the driver's seat, adjusted the rearview mirror and gave them a small salute.

The line ahead of them started to move, and just outside the gates to the school stood their first parade spectators. They looked so happy, sitting in lawn chairs, decked out in their red, white and blue. Flags fluttered on the lampposts all down Main Street. And for the first time since Mom and Dad died, Devin felt connected to his hometown.

His mom had loved all the little celebrations they had in Red Hill Springs. He'd grouse and complain when she made him put on a Santa hat or a patriotic shirt and hauled him down to Main Street, but he'd loved the festivities, too. Mostly he loved hanging out with his friends and gathering up enough candy to fill a pillowcase. But that memory led to his mom, too, with her cool hand on his forehead later when he moaned and groaned with a stomachache.

Lacey nudged him with her elbow. "Where's that signature move? Your fans are waiting."

He shot her a grin from under the brim of his hat, a move he'd made hundreds of times for the cameras, and she laughed.

"There it is. Give the people what they

want." She picked up her hat by the crown and waved it as they passed a few people sitting in their front yard with what looked like a bag of boiled peanuts.

He snickered. "Talk about a signature move."

She gave him a saucy shrug as she placed her hat back on her head. "Just how does this thing end?"

Devin waved to a few kids who were shouting his name and then leaned close to her ear so she could hear him. "At the town square for a barbecue."

As the parade passed, people would walk behind it, or get in their cars and drive to the square. There were inflatables and games for the kids and a band playing music for dancing.

The sun was starting to set as they pulled into the parking lot. The string lights had been turned on over the dance floor and Mayor Grant was there to meet them. She helped Lacey out of the car and said, "You guys are almost off the hook. I'm just going to introduce y'all and then we'll have the opening dance and you'll be released to eat as much barbecue as you like—on the house.

"Wait…dance?" Lacey's feet stalled out and she shot him a get-me-out-of-this look.

"Mayor, I think you and your husband should open the dance floor, as the 'first couple' of Red Hill Springs." Devin looked down at his cane. He wasn't sure exactly how he was going to be able to pull this off.

"It's tradition that the marshal opens the dance floor." Wynn Grant glanced down as she followed his gaze to his cane and her words trailed off. "I mean, unless you don't think you can?"

He had no idea if he could, really, and that fact was galling. "No, I'm fine. Of course we'll do it."

Devin limped onto the stage with Lacey beside him as the remainder of the parade stragglers gathered around. The screams and laughter of kids jumping in the bouncy houses filtered through the band's soft country music.

Wynn tapped the mic and cleared her throat. "Now, some of y'all know that we asked these rodeo sweethearts to be the marshals of the parade at the very last minute and they were nice enough to agree. So, I'd like to introduce four-time world champion barrel racer Lacey Jenkins and three-time world champion saddle bronc rider Devin Cole."

There were some whistles and cheers. Devin took off his hat and gave a little head bow. He held his hand out to Lacey, who curtsied to the crowd.

Mayor Grant said, "I've just learned that Devin and Lacey are newlyweds, so how awesome is it that they'll be opening the dance floor for us tonight?" She half turned to the band. "Take it away, boys."

As the band started to play, Devin wanted to fall straight through the dance floor. He was pretty sure that if there were an award for World Champion of Awkward Moments, he would be sporting a brand-new belt buckle. He painstakingly made his way down the stairs and leaned his cane against the stage.

As he held his hands out to Lacey, he knew she was thinking he'd never turn away from a challenge, even when it was the right thing to do. She had every right to be mad, but she didn't leave him standing there. Instead, she stepped into his arms as the band sang about forever.

He looked into her eyes and smiled, shaken as his memory transported him back to Vegas. The same song was playing, but Lacey'd had a very different look in her eyes then. Instead of wariness, there was trust. Instead of careful conversation, there'd been laughter. Devin had twirled her out and when she spun back into his arms, she'd fit like she belonged there.

He'd blacked out almost everything that happened that night—the night they got married—but this moment he remembered. Because from the time he entered rehab, that dance became his anchor.

The moment *before* he hit rock bottom.

How was it that marrying Lacey was both the best and worst thing he'd ever done? His heart ached, his chest tight with emotion. She was his forever person. He knew it. But he also knew that back then he hadn't owned what it took to stick around.

She knew it, too. And that's why he couldn't be offended that she looked like she'd rather be in a pit of snakes than dance with him in front of the whole town. Or kiss him in the kitchen.

Of course she didn't want to be with him. Because he was definitely the worst decision she'd ever made.

He led her into a twirl under his arm and brought her back in, lacing his fingers with hers with a smile just for her. When she laid her head on his shoulder, he slid his hand up the small of her back and just held her.

Devin didn't know what the future held. But he loved her. That much, at least, he knew.

A firecracker popped a few feet away and as Devin jerked his head around his feet stumbled. Without missing a beat, Lacey caught him, balancing the both of them. And in that second, his resolve stumbled, too.

He could stay sober, but he couldn't fix what was broken. His grandpa used to say, "Devin, you can't make a silk purse out of a sow's ear." As a kid, he'd thought that was ridiculous. Because who wanted a silk purse anyway?

But Devin wanted Lacey to have the silk purse. He wanted her to have everything she needed, the best of everything. As much as he wanted to deny it, he couldn't. He wasn't the best. At anything.

And Lacey deserved so much more.

Chapter Eight

Lacey arranged small bunches of daisies in the buckets lining the bed of the old red Chevy truck. She finished the scene off with a chalkboard sign that indicated two dollars. The weather was warm and humid but the breeze kept it from being oppressive.

Devin was being uncharacteristically quiet. Perched precariously on a step stool, he leaned forward to hang her handmade-quilt-square bunting from the edges of the tin roof.

He wobbled as he reached out with the staple gun, and she flinched. "Maybe we should wait for Garrett to put that up."

"I don't need you to baby me, Lacey. I can put up the bunting without you hovering every second."

She pressed her lips together to keep from

saying what she wanted to say, which was that he was an idiot. Instead, she took a deep breath and tried another tack. "What I mean is that with two sets of hands, it would be easier."

Not to mention safer.

"No."

Okay, then. She mentally raised her hands in defeat as she backed away from the building, but she didn't exhale until Devin had the bunting secured without killing himself.

She gave it a critical eye. "The bunting is really cute. It gives the place the feeling that it's been here awhile. I think the truck needs to come back about a foot, but other than that, once the vegetables are in the bins, we're ready to go."

He got off the step stool, hopping on his good foot until he had his balance. He was so stubborn. "I'll push the truck back."

"Devin, wait. Let Tanner help you." She bit her bottom lip, waiting for the response. She knew her comment wasn't going to go over well.

He shot her a glaring look. "No."

Lacey put herself between Devin and the truck. "Look. I don't know what you're trying to prove, but what you're about to prove is that your ankle can't handle the pressure and you're going to be in so much pain that you won't be able to walk at all."

She gave him the look she'd gotten from her dad a million and one times. The look that said, *you better think before you argue.*

He held her gaze another ten seconds before he dropped his head with a sigh. "I'm sorry. I'm just so…frustrated. I almost fell at the dance last night. I would have if you hadn't caught me."

Hands on hips, she said, "And?"

He shrugged. "I guess I wanted to prove to you that I can do what you need me to do. And I know I can't. I work around the farm all day and do what has to be done, but by the time I get home from my meeting I'm exhausted. My ankle hurts. And I can't sleep."

"Why didn't you say something before now?"

He looked so miserable. "Because I don't know how I'm going to do this."

"What, Dev?" She was so afraid he was going to say be sober. She couldn't imagine how much pain he was in, but she felt like she was seeing the real Devin for the first time and it would kill her to lose him now.

And that thought itself was something she

needed to put away for later. Right now Devin needed her to focus.

"We're about to have two babies. How am I going to help you? I can barely move by nine o'clock at night. And how will I walk a baby? If I have one hand on my cane, I can't pat a baby or even hold it right."

"Devin, no." She shook her head, reaching for him, but he stepped away.

"I'm serious, Lacey. What if I stumble or, God forbid, fall while I'm holding one of them and you're not there to catch me?"

She could think of only one way to allay his fears. Show him that he could do it. "Come in the house with me right now."

"I don't want to go in the house. I'm moving the truck because that's what you said you wanted. So that's what I'm doing." He scowled. "I don't want to talk about this anymore."

"Come in the house. This is more important than the truck." She started for the house without looking back and after a minute she could hear his uneven gait as he followed her across the lawn, grumbling under his breath.

When they got into the house, she went into the kitchen and poured a glass of milk and picked up a cookie from the ones she'd made this morning. She handed him the cookie. "Here. Eat this. I think maybe your blood sugar is low. You're acting kind of hangry."

He narrowed his eyes at her as she started digging through the basket of clothes that Jordan had brought over, but he took a bite.

"I know that thing's in here somewhere." She dumped out the basket. "Ah. Here it is."

She held up a limp loop of fabric. "This is how you hold a baby when you don't have any hands."

"I'm...not sure I'm following you."

"Just give me a second, Devin." He huffed out a breath and she had to smother a giggle. He sounded exactly like his pouty horse when Reggie was miffed about something. "Hold your arms out."

"I thought you wanted me to eat the cookie." She stopped and raised one eyebrow.

He shoved the whole thing in his mouth.

"That's mature. Now hold your arms out."

This time he did as she asked, one corner of his mouth pulling into an unwilling smile.

She held up the wrap. "I watched a video. It's not as hard as it seems." She talked out the steps as she acted them out. "Put the tag in the middle of your stomach. Flip the ends around your back and over the opposite shoulders."

He stared at a spot on the wall behind her. "It would be great if I knew what you were doing."

Muttering to herself, she shoved the ends under the first strap she'd made, crossed them around his back again and tied them in the front, all the while trying not to breathe, as his familiar woodsy scent came up to tickle her nose.

She stepped back and looked. Now that she'd done it, she was kind of skeptical that it would work at all. "I think that's right."

Devin opened his mouth and she put up a finger. "Wait. Just let me try it."

Lacey grabbed a couple of shirts and wadded them up into approximately the size of a newborn baby. She made a pouch from the straps across his front and shoved the baby-shaped figure inside. When she secured the "baby" with the original layer of fabric, his mouth dropped open.

Her gaze went to his.

"Look, Ma, no hands," she whispered.

His eyes were dark pools, his lips tight with emotion.

"You're going to be a great dad, Devin. Having a cane isn't going to change that."

He sucked in a shaky breath, took the wrap

off over his head and tossed it onto the couch. When he spoke, his voice was husky. "What if they're sad that I'm not like other dads? That I can't shag balls for them or run plays in the front yard?"

"Well, first of all, our kids are not doing anything as dangerous as football…" When he snorted a laugh, she felt vindicated. "You're right. You might not be able to do those things… But you can teach them how to fish. You can tell stories about the rodeo and show them how to ride. How to play guitar. Things only you can teach them."

She faced him, holding him by both arms. "Have you ever seen a kid happier than when their daddy's truck pulls up in the driveway? Babies love their mamas but they lose their minds with joy when daddy gets home. That's not about what you do, it's about who you are."

He looked away, his throat working.

Lacey reached down, picked up the glass of milk from the coffee table and handed it to him. "We have a lot to work through, Dev, but I'm not worried about the kind of dad you're going to be. I know you're going to be amazing."

* * *

Devin stood still, the glass in his lax fingers, until he heard the door close behind him. His mind had been buzzing with all the ways he was going to stink as a dad, and she'd answered every one of them with flawless logic.

He was still scared. But maybe he wasn't going to be an utter failure. Maybe he just had to be a little creative.

When he opened the door again, Lacey was sitting in the swing on the front porch with a book. He sat down beside her and toed the swing into motion.

He wanted to say thank you for what she'd said—and done—to help quiet his fears. Instead what came out was, "Your cookies are good."

She gave him a quizzical look, but she smiled. "That makes me happy. Even the colored frosting is all organic, like our produce. I've been thinking we could do flags in July, apples for back to school, pumpkins in the fall, you know, seasonal stuff."

"You're so talented and so creative. Is there anything you've ever done that you're not good at?"

Lacey looked down at her book. She took a quick breath, then paused again before meeting his eyes with a direct, serious look. "I don't think I was a very good friend."

"No, you were a good friend. I was just a really good liar." He sat back and rocked them in silence for a minute, all the tension draining out of his body. "I don't want to lie anymore, Lacey. I don't want to pretend to be something I'm not."

"You don't have to."

He tapped the armrest of the wooden swing with his thumb before saying, "Buck Williams from *Rodeo Roundup* magazine called a few days ago. He wants to do a feature on me and come here to do the interview. I said yes."

Her face flushed and she pushed out of the swing, launching herself to her feet, leaving the pages of her book to flutter in the wind.

"What are you thinking?" he asked.

"I'm not even sure. I want to be happy for you but I'm worried. I'm afraid you haven't given yourself enough time to heal emotionally. And, to be honest, I'm not thrilled about what it means for us when the entire rodeo universe is gossiping about us."

When she turned around, he nodded. "I

understand your concern. And I'm not going to talk about us, I promise. I want—need, really—to share about rehab."

"I'd like some time to process this."

The regaining of his feet wasn't as graceful as hers, but he did it, grabbing his cane from the wall for balance. He walked to the other end of the porch and stood beside her, looking out over the grassy pasture where Reggie casually grazed. "Look, Lacey, I'm not ashamed about this."

He paused. "That's not right. I am, but shame is what keeps people from seeking help. Getting addicted to painkillers after an injury happens a lot. People hide the fact that they're addicted because they think it's a personal failing. In reality, it's much more complicated than that."

Her eyebrows drew together in thought, but still she didn't say anything. And suddenly, he was doubting himself all over again. Doubting *them*. How could it possibly work out with Lacey? She'd acted like she understood him, but maybe she was just waiting for him to fail. Or maybe she'd never had any intention of trying to make things work.

But that was the fear talking again. He remembered the way she'd wrapped the baby sling around him a few minutes ago and released the breath he'd been holding. "I promise you this. Doing the interview is not about fame and it's not about getting back in the game. It's about letting other people like me know they're not alone."

Her hand was on her stomach, where their babies were growing, and tears gathered in her eyes. "Okay. If this is important to you, then I support you. When is he coming?"

"Tomorrow."

Devin paced the floor inside the farmhouse as he waited for the reporter to arrive. He'd done hundreds of interviews, but none of them had been as important, or as tricky, as this one would be.

He hadn't seen Lacey this morning. He wasn't surprised. Being with him came with a whole lot of baggage that she didn't want to unpack in public. And honestly, he didn't blame her.

In his mind, he ran over the points he wanted to make as he answered questions about his time in rehab. Even though he'd been waiting for it, the knock surprised him.

He took a deep breath, said his millionth prayer and pulled open the door.

"Buck! Man, I've missed you." Devin gave his friend a one-armed hug.

"I've missed you, too. I don't have nearly as much fun now that you're retired. That is, if you're retired?" Buck gave him a speculative look.

"There's no such thing as small talk with you. I forgot about that." Devin laughed. He and Buck had become good friends before one too many concussions had taken Buck out of the competition and into the press. "I thought maybe we could sit outside. You want something to drink?"

"No thanks, I'm good." Buck followed Devin to a small grouping of chairs with a small table between them. As they got seated, he gave the landscape an appreciative look. "It's beautiful here. I can see why you want to be home."

"I'm partial to it." Buck was right. It was a gorgeous summer day. The sky was so wide and so blue, with huge, fluffy white clouds. The trees and the grass brilliant green, not yet faded by the harsh summer sun.

"Thanks for agreeing to do the interview."

Nerves twisted up in Devin's stomach again but he refused to back away from this.

The cost of pretending to be something that he wasn't was too high. So he nodded.

Buck pulled out a tape recorder and laid it on the table. "Okay?"

Devin nodded again. "I'm ready."

The door opened and Lacey walked out onto the porch. She dressed casually in faded jeans and a T-shirt and not a lot of makeup. But her hair tumbled in loose waves around her shoulders and her pregnancy was undeniable.

He appreciated what she was trying to do, but once their relationship was out?

There was no going back.

Chapter Nine

Lacey stood in the open doorway. Joining Devin's interview had seemed like a good idea when she'd thought of it before she went to sleep last night. As she stood here, about to blow their lives wide-open, it didn't seem so smart.

But then she got a look at Devin's flabbergasted face and she knew she was doing the right thing. Because they might have the weirdest marriage in history—and she doubted that—but she'd been his friend first. From here on out, she was going to remember that.

He stood as she stepped onto the porch and closed the door behind her, intercepting her before she could get to Buck. "What are you doing?"

Her gaze locked on his. "Joining your interview."

"Are you sure you want to do this?"

"One hundred percent." So, the number was actually hovering around 40 percent, but Devin didn't need to know that.

Buck's gaze bounced from one of them to the other. "Uh, hey, Lacey."

She gave him a warm hug. "Surprised to see me?"

Buck was still obviously reeling because he was having trouble finding words. "Yeah, I mean, I'd heard rumors that the two of you were together in Vegas, but no one had any evidence of that being true. Until now... I guess?"

"That's outside the scope of this interview. I'm sorry, Buck, but my relationship with Lacey has to be off the record. I want to be transparent about what I'm going through, but Lacey isn't a part of that."

She laid her hand over his, threading her fingers through his. "It's okay, Devin. I'm not trying to hide our relationship."

"So," the reporter said slowly. "You two are..."

"Married." Lacey squeezed Devin's hand. "And pregnant. With twins."

Buck burst out laughing. "I have to hand it to you. You two never do anything halfway." He paused, then looked at Devin, a question in his eyes. "So, she's the reason you went to rehab."

At the same moment Lacey said no, Devin said a firm *yes*.

The word hit her like a blow. "Yes?"

"Yes." He draped his arm across the back of the seat. "She's the reason I went. But she's not the reason I stayed."

Buck smiled and made a note on his pad. "What did make you stay?"

"I knew there were things in my life I didn't deal with. A lot of things, actually. I'd stuffed it down for years, and riding broncs and partying helped with that. But it got bad enough that what I was going to lose was more painful than just dealing with it."

"And did you deal with it?" Buck's question, true to form, was direct.

"Yeah. It's ongoing." Devin's smile tipped up. "Staying sober is a little harder. It means making that choice every day. Every minute sometimes."

"And are you planning a return to rodeo?"

Devin paused. Following his gaze, Lacey knew he was looking at Reggie out in the pasture. The two of them had been an indomitable team. It had to be painful to know you'd never experience that again.

The silence stretched. Finally, Devin looked Buck square in the eyes. "No. I won't be back. I'm grateful for all the fans and everyone who made this part of my life so amazing." He glanced at Lacey. "But my ankle injury took me out of contention and, to be honest, my priorities are a little different now."

A half an hour later, Buck closed his pad and stuck his pencil through the wire closure. "Frankly, I'm glad to see the two of you finally together. Mind if we walk around a little? I'd love to get some photos of you guys before it gets too hot."

So Devin showed Buck around the farm, Lacey's hand firmly in his grip. And for just a while, it felt like old times, like maybe they didn't have so many unresolved questions between them. It gave her a glimpse of how it could be between them on the other side.

She was still so confused about what she wanted. She knew Devin should be involved in the lives of the twins—she'd grown up without a mom and she'd missed that. She wouldn't do that to her babies. But beyond that, she just didn't know.

Being with Devin was so confusing. Despite her anger and hurt, she'd never stopped having feelings for him. She just didn't know what those feelings were, exactly. And she definitely didn't know where she wanted to go with them. Or even if she wanted to go somewhere with them. Loving Devin and trusting him were two very different things.

Buck stopped them by the pasture where Reggie was spending his retirement. "Let's take one right here by the fence. Face each other so the people can see that baby belly, Lacey."

Warmth rushed into her cheeks, but she did as he asked.

"Now, I want to see a kiss."

"Nope." Devin's response was quick and firm. But his arm snaked out and he pulled her toward him. She laughed as her balance shifted. He put his hand over hers on her belly to help her stay upright and he kissed her on the forehead.

Her throat tight, she took a step back, but she left her hand on his. For years, she'd dreamed that one day Devin would look at her like that, with his heart in his eyes. She wished she could be sure that it was real and not just Devin still hiding what really was instead of sharing the truth.

As Buck packed up his camera, they walked him back to his rental car. Devin paused, his arm around Lacey. She was aware—too aware—of the warmth of his fingers curled around her waist.

Devin picked up the conversation. "I just want to say this before you go, Buck. I did this interview because addiction is something a lot of people try to keep in the dark. That's twenty-one million Americans trying to hide their substance abuse problem."

Buck nodded. "What do you want to say to people who might be struggling?"

"It's time to bring it to the light. Having to ask for help is not something to be ashamed of. It's not a weakness." He glanced at the barn, where it seemed he could see his dad in the entrance. Boots on. Sleeves rolled up. Dusty hat.

A lump formed in Devin's throat and he swallowed hard. "My dad used to say strength doesn't come from doing what you already know you can do. Real strength comes from overcoming things you never thought you could."

"That's the wisdom of experience right

there. And it's a good word." Buck shook Devin's hand. "Thanks, man. Lacey, anything you want to add?"

Her shoulders trembled and Devin pulled her tighter against his side. She looked up at him as she spoke. "Just that… I'm proud of Devin. What he's doing is hard, and instead of trying to pretend his life is perfect, he's sharing what he's been through so other people don't have to feel so alone."

Devin cleared his throat as Buck pinched the bridge of his nose between his fingers. "Now y'all have gone and made me cry. Thanks a lot. I hope I'll be able to do this justice, Dev. It was really great to see y'all. Now I've got to go so I don't miss my plane." Buck got in his car and slammed the door, sending them a little wave as he drove down the driveway.

For a moment, they just stood and watched Buck drive away. They'd done hundreds of interviews together, but this felt different— was different.

Devin sighed. "Well, that's done. Nowhere left to hide. I feel both relieved and nauseous."

She nudged him with her shoulder. "That sounds about right to me. And I meant it when I said I was proud of you."

"You being there made it easier. Better."
He waved a hand, as if he could wave away
the emotion that all the talking had dredged
up. "Come on, let's go find a cup of coffee."

Lacey turned back to the house, Devin's
arm still around her waist. She should step
away—she knew she should—but the peace
between them at this moment was too good
to let go of just yet.

A gust of wind came out of nowhere, her
hair whipping around her face. When she
could finally see again, she realized Devin
was focused on something over her shoulder.

She turned around to look. The clouds were
dark and building, their color ranging from
charcoal to ashy gray. "That doesn't look
good."

"I don't know which way that's going but
it looks like the bottom's about to fall out."

Tanner came roaring down the lane in the
all-terrain vehicle they used for farm work.
He stopped beside them and jumped out.
"There's a whole line of storms moving in
from the gulf and the fence is down in the
back field. Half the cows are out and one of
them just dropped twins. I have to get the
cows in and fix the fence before we lose our
stock in this storm."

As he spoke, he walked into the barn, Devin right behind him. Lacey squinted toward the south just as a lightning bolt streaked across the sky.

"I'm going with you." Devin grabbed rain gear from the tack room and shrugged into it.

"I'll take care of it." Tanner grabbed the toolbox and went right back out the door.

Devin followed him. "I can help."

Tanner slid into the seat of the ATV and cranked it up. "I have enough to worry about out there. I can't be responsible for you, too."

He didn't wait for an answer, just whipped the vehicle into a turn and drove off.

Devin walked through the barn to the door that led to the pasture. He stuck his finger and thumb into his mouth and let out a piercing whistle, calling Reggie.

Lacey didn't try to stop Devin. She knew if she wasn't pregnant she'd be saddling up, too. Tanner needed help whether he wanted to accept it or not. And while Devin was injured, Tanner couldn't ask for a better team than Devin and Reggie to have his back.

With Reggie tacked up and ready to go, Devin stuck his good foot in the stirrup and swung his other leg over the saddle. Reggie sidestepped as Devin settled in the saddle, and Lacey wasn't sure if the big horse was excited to be going out or nervous because of the storm.

"You'll get inside?" Devin pulled his hat down over his eyes as thunder crashed. "I've got to go."

Rain pelted the tin roof of the barn. She raised her voice over the noise. "I'll be fine. Go."

She watched him ride out of the barn into the storm, lowering his head against the wind and the rain, and looking like some kind of hero out of an old-timey cowboy movie.

Lightning streaked the sky, splitting into multiple veins and racing to the ground. She picked up his cane and sprinted for the house, completely drenched by the time she reached the porch. She shook the water out of her hair and opened the door, pausing to look back, down the road.

Devin was out of sight, but he wouldn't be out of her mind. She'd be praying nonstop until he and Tanner returned to the house safe and sound.

Devin couldn't see through the driving rain. He wound through the woods behind the field. He'd caught sight of Tanner trying to bolster the fence as he'd passed the field. The cows were strewn from here to the property line.

He understood why Tanner said what he did. Devin wasn't mad. He just knew that if he was going to stay here on the farm, things weren't going to work that way. Devin may be injured but he had to be useful. If he wasn't, he may as well give up.

Besides, all discussion about his skills aside, Reggie was the best cow horse Devin had ever seen. It would be criminal not to let him use his talents.

Reggie didn't hesitate. He knew exactly what to do to get the cows to move the direction Devin wanted them to go. And when one cow started moving, others noticed and started to tag along. The new mama with her calf was under a tree near the fence line and Devin turned her back toward the other cow. "Come on, Mama, you know you want to go home."

Thunder rumbled in the distance. He couldn't tell if the storm was coming or going. But the rain had slacked off, leaving the farm in a kind of quasi dusk, just enough light that he could see another cow with one of the older spring calves wandering off. He nudged Reggie to go after the cow, running just even with her until she saw him.

She was stubborn and took a few more steps the other way, but Devin moved Reggie slowly forward until the cow acknowledged she wasn't going on a walkabout tonight and slowly turned back to join the rest of the small herd.

Their stock was valuable. They couldn't afford to lose even one. He rode the back of the herd until they found Tanner finishing up the repairs on the fence. Devin sidled up to Tanner as the cattle turned into the pasture, moseying in their no-hurry way. Tanner, his hands encased in yellow leather gloves, used the pliers to attach the wire fencing to the post. He'd have to come back out tomorrow to make sure it held and that it was secure. But for tonight, it would keep the cows where they belonged.

Tanner made a final twist with the pliers and looked up at Devin. Raindrops were hitting his face and clinging to his lashes but he didn't seem to notice. "I could've done it without you."

"You're welcome." Devin tamped down his annoyance. Tanner was on his own path.

Tanner took his hat off and rubbed his

sleeve across his eyes. "We're missing one of the new calves. He's a twin and Mom was rejecting him. He doesn't stand a chance out there alone. Want to help me look?"

"What color is he?"

"Chocolate brown, some white on the face." Tanner looked into the field where the cows were acting like they'd never left. "There's another storm right behind this one. We're not gonna have long."

"Let's go." Devin clucked to Reggie and wheeled around, heading back into the rangy pines while Tanner cranked up the ATV. Visibility was terrible, rain still dripping from the sky and the trees, the clouds dark and ominous.

They split up, Tanner starting on one end of the pasture in the ATV, Devin on the other on horseback, searching to the property line until they met in the middle. He yelled to Tanner, "Anything?"

"No sign. You up for another pass?"

"We're not leaving him out here, so yeah."

This time they worked out from the center, and about five minutes into the second search, Devin heard Tanner yell. He turned Reggie and met Tanner coming back toward him, carrying the calf in his arms. He was tiny and limp. Devin wasn't even sure he was breathing. "Is he alive?"

"I think so. Barely. We need to get him warm and dry and fed. Can you take him in while I check the rest of the fence?"

"Of course."

Tanner handed the little cow up to Devin, who laid him gently across his lap. "I'll take care of him."

He nudged Reggie with his heels. "Let's go, bud."

As Reggie picked up the pace, the little calf didn't move. Devin rubbed his neck with one hand. "Come on, baby, you can make it. You're tough."

Devin was exhilarated and exhausted by the time he wheeled Reggie into the barn. He slid off the horse and onto his good foot, hopping a little until he could stand. The calf slid right off and into his arms. Devin laid him gently onto a blanket and then quickly untacked Reggie, lifting the saddle off last and putting it over the saddle stand in the tack room.

Lacey had clearly been back in the barn because there was fresh hay and feed in the largest stall. She was always thinking about the other person. He was torn between wanting to yell at her for going back out in the storm and wanting to kiss her for knowing he would be exhausted.

He led Reggie into the stall and gave him a good rub before closing the door. "You've still got it, old man."

Lifting the calf into his arms, he struggled to his feet. Every step was agony on his wrecked ankle. Since he didn't have a choice, he just kept taking steps, one at a time, until he was at the door to the house.

Lacey was there opening it before he could even try to figure out how he was going to knock. She pulled him into the house, getting her shoulder underneath his and wrapping her arm around his waist for support. "Is he okay?"

"Don't know." Devin was out of breath. "Mama rejected him and he's wet and cold. Dehydrated, too, probably."

He laid the calf on the rug in the living room and rubbed the small face between his palms.

Lacey ran to the laundry room and came back with an armful of towels, warm from the dryer. She knelt beside Devin, handing him a towel. She used another as a blanket and a third to begin drying the baby's hindquarters. "Do you have colostrum?"

He glanced up at her. "Yeah. There's a cabinet in the laundry room where Tanner keeps all the meds. We've got a couple of bottles and the milk replacer on the bottom shelf."

"I know what to do. I've raised at least a dozen bottle babies in my time. You go get dry before you get sick, too."

Devin looked up ruefully. "Do you know where my cane is?"

Asking her for it was hard enough, and to her credit, she made no comment, just handed him his cane from the corner of the room. With the cane taking his weight, he slowly gained his feet. "Thanks, Lacey."

At his side, she turned her face to his. "When you get through changing, I made some taco soup. It's warming on the stove."

He stared into her brown eyes, so clear and expressive. If things had been different, he would have pulled her close and kissed her until those beautiful eyes melted on his.

She put a hand to her hair. "What? Do I have something on my face?"

Devin shook his head. "No. I just like being with you. That's all."

A silence hung in the living room, except

for the sound of the rain on the roof and the soup simmering on the stove. Lacey put her hand to his cheek, caressing it with her thumb. She hesitated, maybe afraid to say something she would regret. Finally, she said, "I like being with you, too."

If wishes were fishes, his mother used to say. She would never finish her sentence. If wishes were fishes…*what*? He'd said that often enough to her as he was growing up. She would shrug with a smile and tell him one day he would understand. She was right. Now he knew. Fish were plentiful. Wishes coming true, not so much.

With his slow, halting gait, he started up the stairs. If he was blessed enough that one of those wishes came true, it would be that Lacey would trust him with her heart.

Because if he had another chance, he would guard it with his life.

Chapter Ten

Lacey roused slowly, feeling like she was climbing out of a deep hole and someone was bumping her legs as she tried to climb. She squinched her eyes tightly closed, waving the person away with a grumble. "Stop it—I'm tired."

She started climbing again but the nudges to her legs continued. Struggling to a seated position on the couch, she opened her eyes and looked down. Big dark brown eyes with the longest lashes she'd ever seen blinked at her before a smooth, wet tongue streaked out and wrapped around her wrist.

"Hi, baby." Laughing, she leaned forward and scratched the calf between the ears and under the chin. He reminded her of a puppy—

a really, really big puppy—wanting to play. "Oh, you are cute. You remind me of Sadie."

Hearing her name, the dog lifted her head, then laid it back down with a subtle groan. Yeah, it had been a long night, but the little calf was standing on wobbly legs and bumping her knees with his head, trying to get her to feed him. Thank goodness. One more thump from the calf's nose and Lacey began the process of heaving her off-balance body to stand up. "Okay, okay. I'm getting up."

Thunder rumbled in the distance and, through the half-closed blinds, Lacey caught a glimpse of the pearl-gray sky. So, the storms were still rolling through. Neither she nor Devin had gotten much sleep. They'd put the little calf on one of Sadie's dog beds. He'd been so weak he couldn't lift his head, much less have the strength to drink from a bottle. It had been so rushed and so touch-and-go that they hadn't even wanted to name him.

She and Devin had taken turns giving him "doses" of colostrum with a turkey baster and Sadie had mothered him, too, licking his face and cleaning him up. Lacey had taken a deep breath and girded herself for the heartbreak of his not making it through the night. She was so happy she'd been wrong.

He'd apparently gotten enough calories for a jump start because he was now trying to munch her fingers, looking for one that would feed him.

Lacey pushed to her feet as Devin stepped out of the kitchen, carrying tongs and wearing a bright red apron. "I thought I heard some noise out here. Well, how about that? Nemo is up."

"Nemo?"

"We were bonding in the middle of the night and I had to call him something. He was lost and we had to find him? Get it?" He pointed the tongs at her. "You wanna try to do better?"

"Nope. I'm good with it. But just so you know, I'm naming the babies." The calf butted her in the backside. "We better get Nemo a bottle before he has a meltdown."

He grinned. "Already got one made. I was feeling hopeful."

"I'll check on breakfast while you try the bottle. I don't want him to decide he needs to head-butt the babies."

"Oh, good thought. The spoon for the grits is by the stove."

"Got it." She lifted the lid to the pot and backed away from the steam before giving it a stir. "I've never had a calf in the house, but I'm an expert at bottle-feeding. My dad doesn't believe in feeders, so we always had at least a few bottle babies each season."

Tanner stepped into the kitchen from the back porch, taking off his wet hat. "Hand-feeding is better. It doesn't last long and the calves are healthier. He looks like he's getting his strength back."

Devin held the bottle where Nemo could reach it and turned to the side so he wouldn't get head-butted in a sensitive area. She grinned. Seemed like Devin had some experience with bottle-feeding calves, as well.

Tanner knelt down and when Nemo grabbed hold of the teat, he steadied the calf's head so he could stay latched on. Nemo sucked down the bottle in about two minutes flat and knocked into Devin's hip, wanting more.

"So here's a question—where are we going to put him now that he's on his feet?" Tanner looked up from where he knelt on the floor. "Any thoughts?"

"He needs a bib."

"That's your thought?" Tanner blinked seriously.

Lacey tossed him a dishrag, which he used

to wipe the little cow's slobbery mouth. When Tanner thought she wasn't looking, he gave Nemo a rub behind the ears before standing up. Lacey smiled to herself. *I see you, tough guy.*

"These are almost ready." She took the lid off the pot of grits and stirred it again from the bottom, fixing her gaze on Devin. "What if we put him in the ring next to the barn?"

Devin shrugged. "It could work. We're going to have to get the calf a buddy of some kind or he's going to be lonely...and loud."

"No more animals." Tanner pointed to himself. "Not Noah," he said, then gestured to the barn. "Not an ark. I mean it, Devin. He can have Sadie."

The dog, who'd moved her sleeping position from the living room to under the kitchen table, huffed softly as she heard her name. Tanner patted her head. "See, she's already looking forward to it."

He grabbed a biscuit with ham from the pan where they were warming. "Put the calf in the laundry room on the dog bed until we're sure he's stable and then we'll move him outside."

"When it stops raining," Lacey interjected into the conversation, then immediately felt like she should turn around and see who gave that order to Devin's brother.

Tanner stopped and stared at her for a few seconds. Long enough for Devin to notice and look up, his eyes traveling from Tanner to Lacey and back again.

"When it stops raining," Tanner conceded.

She smiled. "Perfect. No grits for you?"

"No, I'm going to take the opportunity since it's raining to pay some bills." He grimaced. "Or open some bills, anyway. Which reminds me, Devin, there's a stack of mail that's been piling up on my desk for you. Can you come and get it?"

"Coming." Devin picked up his cane, leaned toward Lacey and stage-whispered. "I want grits."

She elbowed him. "I know. Can one of you take the calf to the laundry room on your way out, please?"

Tanner picked up the calf with a grunt. "He's going outside as soon as it stops raining." In answer, Nemo laid his head on Tanner's shoulder.

Lacey pressed her lips together. Tanner was toast. He didn't even have a chance against those long brown eyelashes. And the calf? She was pretty sure it already thought it was a dog. With quick, efficient motions, she loaded their bowls with grits and sprinkled cheese over the top. She put a ham biscuit on the plate with some of the melon she'd cut up last night while the guys had been out searching for the calf.

Devin came back with a stack of mail that he tossed on the table. "I'm starving. That looks delicious, thank you."

They ate quietly, Devin tucking into the grits like he'd never seen food before. Lacey ate her grits and biscuit and sat back, sipping her single cup of coffee.

Devin picked up his mug and leaned back in his chair, shoulders slumping. "I'm exhausted. How much do you think we were up last night?"

"I don't know. We were both awake until around four, I think. I passed out on the couch after that. Did you sleep at all?"

"About an hour, I think, maybe two, if you count dozing in between trying to feed Nemo."

"I'm so tired." Lacey stared blankly at a spot on the wall. "This is what the next year of our life is going to be like."

"At least. What about when they're teenagers? We can't sleep then."

She turned wide eyes on him. "I didn't know night before last was the last time I'd get to sleep for eighteen years. I should've enjoyed it more."

Devin laughed. "I have an idea... We'll take turns sleeping."

Lacey looked down into her mug. Joking with Devin reminded her of how things used to be. As much as she loved it, she couldn't take things for granted anymore. He was trying, but they had a long way to go before she would trust that he would stay if things got hard. And things would get hard.

He'd been the life of the party and the darling of the rodeo circuit for the last five years. She'd been in love with him longer than that. But when he left her in that hotel room alone, it broke something between them. Something she wasn't sure she could get back.

She took a deep breath, drained her remaining coffee and pushed away from the table. Sitting here, laughing with Devin... It was a little too much like actually being married. And that realization just made things hurt worse.

Devin's smile slowly faded. He didn't know what happened. One second they'd been commiserating about the state of their sleep for the next eighteen years, and the next she was contemplating the bottom of her coffee mug as if it held the secrets of the universe.

But that wasn't exactly true. He did know what happened. She was scared. And it was because of him. He just wished it didn't cause an ache in his heart every time she pulled away from him.

He grabbed the pile of mail and tried to focus. If he didn't sort through it, Tanner would be disappointed in him. And he was doing everything possible to make sure that didn't happen.

He flipped through the envelopes.

There were a few small outstanding bills he needed to pay. A request from an acquaintance—someone who hadn't been notified of Devin's change in circumstances—for a donation to charity.

And a flier from the hospital. "Hey, what's this?"

He pulled the sticker loose and unfolded the paper. "Magnificent Multiples class. Cool. It says here they cover must-know topics such as crib safety, choosing a car seat, scheduling—do babies really have schedules?" When she didn't answer, he went on. "Also what to expect in labor and delivery and a tour of the hospital. It says here, not mandatory but strongly recommended. Do you want me to sign us up?"

Devin glanced up. Lacey's face had gone white. "Lacey?"

She blinked, shuddered and focused her eyes on him. "I can't go to that."

Devin studied her face. He knew she was not a fan of hospitals, to say the least, but this was just a class. "They're just gonna teach us how to make a bottle and change a diaper. No big deal."

"The class is at the hospital."

He frowned at the paper. "Well, yeah, but looking at the map here, it's barely in the door."

"I'm not doing it." She stood, picked up their plates and dumped them in the sink.

"I don't think they're gonna tell you the delivery is off if we don't go, but it says here that they strongly encourage participation."

She didn't say anything to that, just turned on the water and started washing the dishes to load them in the dishwasher.

Devin stood up, grabbed his cane and walked over behind her, putting his hands on her shoulders. Her muscles were concrete. "Lacey, talk to me."

Instead of answering him, she spun, walking away from him, out of the kitchen and straight out the front door.

He braced himself with both hands on the counter. Lacey was one of the most self-confident people he'd ever met. She never hesitated to reach for the brass ring. And she should know this class was necessary.

With a sigh, he flipped on the electric kettle and picked up where she left off rinsing the dishes in the sink. Okay, so she was freaked out by hospitals. He knew that. He'd sworn often enough not to let the EMTs take her to one unless her life was hanging in the balance. He just didn't know why.

Putting the last dish in the dishwasher, he closed it up and turned it on. No matter what was motivating Lacey's fear, he knew her and he had to believe she was afraid of the hospital for a good reason.

The only problem he could see—and it was a big one—was that she was going to have to give birth at some point.

With his cane in one hand and a mug of herbal tea in the other, he made his way to the front porch. Rain dripped from the eaves, dark clouds still swirling in the sky.

Lacey was sitting in the chair at the far end of the porch, where they'd had their interview with Buck. Was that just yesterday?

It seemed like a lifetime ago.

"Hey." He approached her slowly and held out the mug. "Sorry it's not coffee."

"Thanks." She took the mug. "Wanna sit?"

He eased down next to her on the love seat, put his arm across her shoulders and studied the rain. "I'm not going to pretend that I understand what's going on in your head right now."

Lacey's head dropped back against his arm and she sighed. "Probably for the best."

"So, I'm not trying to state the obvious, but sooner or later, we're most likely going to have to go to the hospital at some point."

"I know." Her voice was small and quiet, so unlike her that he looked down at her again.

"What if I make the reservations? Going for the class might be a good way to test the waters. And when you're ready to talk about it, *if* you're ready to talk about it, I'll be here."

"I don't think the waters are going to be very inviting, but we can try."

"Yeah?" When she nodded, he hugged her

closer to him. "I say we stop talking about the bad place and discuss what we're going to name our little team ropers, since the big ultrasound is coming up this week and apparently you don't think I'm good at naming things."

"You're not." She didn't even try to hide her laugh. "Do you think they're boys or girls?"

"Well, they can be team ropers either way, but I'm calling boys."

She shook her head. "Nah, I'm pretty sure they're girls."

Devin scoffed at that. "Have you seen me and my brothers? We don't have girls in our family."

"Guess we'll see."

"Guess we will."

She tapped his knee. "If you're right, I'll make breakfast every day for a week."

He raised an eyebrow, his eyes narrowing into a speculative squint. "I get to sleep in?"

"If you're right. Which you're not."

"Okay, so say I'm wrong…"

She grinned. "You have to rub my feet every day for a week."

"Deal. But full disclosure… I'd rub your feet anyway."

"You would?"

"Of course." That she didn't know he would do absolutely anything for her made him feel like a heel. The silence between them stretched. He'd been so focused on "winning" her back that he really hadn't stopped to think about how she actually felt.

Not the part about being mad at him, but the part where she was pregnant and married and nothing was normal for her. At all. "You know, Lace, I've never been where you are, but I bet you feel alone in all this and I do know what that feels like."

She looked up at him and gave her head a small shake. "It's silly to feel alone when I'm here with you and Tanner."

"You can be in the middle of a crowd of people and still feel alone. I know because I lived it. And when you have secrets, you feel like there's a wall between you and the rest of the world."

Her eyes were huge and dark and tears gathered. "I do feel like that sometimes. I want to share this—all of this—with you, Devin. It's why I stayed. I'm just not fully there yet. I'm trying."

"I know you are. I'm trying, too." There was a hot knot of emotion in his chest and he swallowed hard. "If you need anything—

sheesh, this sounds cheesy—but if you need *anything*, I'd be honored if you'd let me help you."

She giggled and rubbed the tears from under her eyes with her thumb and finger. "It does sound cheesy, but thanks. I'm already huge. I have a feeling I'm going to need a lot of help in the next few months."

"I'm here for it."

"I know." She turned her gaze to the pasture, where the grass was glistening in the rain. "How about Prudence for a girl? My first horse's name was Prudence. I really loved that horse."

Devin closed his eyes, rapidly running the scenarios through his mind. One, she was joking and he should laugh. Two, she wasn't joking and if he laughed, her feelings would be hurt. Three… Wait a minute. Her shoulders were shaking. He grinned. "I love Prudence. And it's precious that you would name our baby after your first horse. I'm thinking Elmo for a boy."

She stopped laughing. "Like the fast-food joint or the fuzzy red puppet with the annoying voice?"

"Well, I was thinking of the hamburger

place, but now that you mention it, that puppet is downright adorable."

She sat up and glanced back at him from under her lashes. "I'm so glad I know you're kidding. I'm going in to check on Nemo and then, if you don't mind, I'm going to take a nap."

"I don't mind at all. I'll wake you up when lunch is ready."

"Thanks, Devin." She took a few steps toward the door before turning back. "And thanks for not pressuring me to talk and just being with me. I appreciate it."

"Anytime." When the door closed behind her, he laid his head back against the chair. Their relationship was so tricky. And he was sure he was messing it up every day.

But God had brought him through the worst of his addiction and was with him every single day. He knew God was with him and with Lacey and their babies, too, even through all the confusion.

He wanted everything to be okay with Lacey. He would say he wanted to have the relationship they had before, but that wasn't it. He wanted this relationship. The one they had right now. The one they were building on mutual trust and respect.

And he trusted that God could take what they offered and build them into a family.

His phone rang in his pocket and he looked at the readout. It was Lacey. "Hello?"

"I'm thinking Gomer, like Gomer Pyle, for a boy. I bet he'd be the only Gomer in his kindergarten class."

"I think you are sleep deprived and you need a nap." The last thing he heard before the phone went dead in his ear was her laughing. He chuckled to himself, shaking his head.

His wife was resilient and spunky and beautiful. She was going to be an amazing mother to their babies.

Baby boys... He was sure of it.

He couldn't wait for the ultrasound—not because he wanted to sleep in, but because every step in this wacky journey they were taking brought him closer to his babies and closer to Lacey. And that was exactly where he wanted to be.

Chapter Eleven

The lights were dim in the exam room. The only sound was the tapping of the technician's fingers on the keys of the computer. Lacey'd had an ultrasound when the doctor first suspected she was carrying twins, of course, but this one was different.

This time Devin sat at her shoulder, wide eyes glued to the monitor, mouth slightly open. He was so into it and she loved seeing his excitement.

The tech moved the wand across her stomach. "So we're almost finished with measurements for Baby A. Oh, here's the little face."

It was a blur of light and shadow, but Lacey could make out eyes and a nose and a mouth. As they watched, the baby rubbed its hand across its cheek. Devin didn't speak, but he slid his hand down her arm and linked his fingers with hers.

"And you want to know the gender?"

"Yes." Lacey glanced up at Devin. He had a twinkle in his eye. She knew he was thinking about the little game they had going.

Once again, the tech moved the wand around, zooming in and out until she stopped and pointed to the screen. "Well, guys, congratulations, Baby A is a boy."

"Yes!" Devin grinned and did a little I-was-right boogie. "I knew it. You're cooking breakfast every day for a week."

Lacey shook her head. He was so predictable. And so ridiculously cute. How was she supposed to use her brain and make wise decisions when he looked at her like that?

"And let's go to Baby B…" The ultrasound technician guided the wand into position. "Baby B is definitely *not* a boy."

"It's a girl?" Lacey's hand crept up to cover her mouth. She looked up at Devin. "One of each okay with you, cowboy?"

"It's one of each." His voice was delighted, his eyes tender as he looked down at her. "I don't know why we never considered that combination."

"Ah, there's Baby B's face. She looks like

she's sucking her thumb." The tech pointed to the screen. "And I could be wrong but it looks like she has a dimple."

Devin laughed. "Perfect."

Lacey watched as the technician took the measurements for Baby B, shadows and light stretching and fading on the screen, but she didn't really know what she was seeing. Boy or girl… It was fun to joke and guess, but she really just wanted to know they looked healthy. "They're okay?"

The tech shot her a distracted smile as she continued the scan until finally, with a few more spins of the roller ball on the ultrasound machine and clicking of measurements, they were finished.

The tech handed her a cloth to wipe her stomach. "Dr. Lescale's going to look over the video and she'll be in to visit with you. You can get dressed."

She left the room, turning the light on as she closed the door behind her.

That wasn't quite an answer.

While Devin waited outside, Lacey dressed quickly, nerves overtaking her stomach. Was the tech not supposed to tell them anything? What if something was wrong?

Dr. Lescale entered the room, laughing

at something Devin had said. Surely she wouldn't be laughing if something were wrong with their babies.

Lacey sat in the chair next to Devin, her hands twisted in her lap, as the doctor sanitized and pulled the computer monitor toward her, sliding on her glasses.

After a moment, Dr. Lescale glanced up, looking at them over the top of her reading glasses. "Babies look great. Tracking just right size-wise for their gestational age of twenty weeks. Baby A is a little bit smaller, but that's not unusual. Any questions?"

"They're okay?" Lacey's eyes filled, and she blinked back the tears. "I don't know why, I just all of a sudden got worried."

The doctor picked up a tissue and handed it to her. "Completely normal to have some nerves, especially on a big day like today. But I don't see anything that concerns me. All the signs I look for are good. One thing to be aware of is that it's very rare for twins to go to forty weeks. That's nothing to worry about. Babies born beyond thirty-two weeks normally do very well."

Lacey blinked, suddenly feeling like there was an anvil on her chest. She could possibly have only twelve more weeks of pregnancy to go?

The doctor looked between the two of them. "Any questions so far?"

Lacey looked at Devin. "You have any questions?"

He hesitated. "Yeah. I just want to know... When is the crying going to start?"

Lacey and Dr. Lescale both swung around to stare at him. "Crying?"

Devin shifted uneasily in his chair.

Lacey wanted to be supportive, but inside she was still reeling from the timeline bombshell. She just kept thinking twelve weeks... twelve weeks...twelve weeks. How was that even possible?

"When we were here last time, in the waiting room there was a pregnant lady and she just cried nonstop. Her husband said she'd been crying for weeks."

To Dr. Lescale's credit, she didn't even snicker, just reached across and patted Devin on the hand. "I think you're in the clear on that one. Crying without ceasing is not a normal part of being pregnant."

"Oh, what a relief. I mean, I'm here for it, Lacey. Whatever it is. Even crying."

Lacey shared a look with the doctor, who

smiled and made a notation on a sheet of paper and handed it to Lacey.

"I'll see you in one month, before that if you have any concerns."

The door closed behind the doctor and Lacey slumped in the chair. The babies could be here in as little as twelve weeks.

And she still didn't have the foggiest idea what happened after that.

Devin cranked up the truck, shooting Lacey a sideways glance. She'd been so quiet on the walk to the parking lot. "Talk to me. What's going on in your head?"

"I don't want to talk right now, Devin. I just need to figure stuff out."

He started to put the car into gear and then stopped. "No. You don't. Or, to be more exact, you don't have to figure it out on your own. Talk to me."

"Fine. You want me to talk, here goes. If things were different, we wouldn't have to hurry this. We could take our time and we would know if… We would know if this could work out."

"You mean, we would know if I'm going to stay sober."

She lifted her chin. "Yes, partly."

"What's the other part?"

"We don't know *anything*, Devin. We're not just pregnant. There are *actual* twins in here. Actual babies. And in twelve weeks, they could be here and I'm going to be responsible for them." Her voice broke on a sob and she buried her face in her hands.

Devin froze. So, Dr. Lescale had apparently been wrong about the crying. He put his hand on Lacey's shoulder and gave her an awkward pat. "It's gonna be okay, Lace."

She turned on him, her face flushed, eyes flashing angrily. "How can you say that? We don't have anything ready. Nothing. We don't even have names picked out. We're living with your brother!"

Her voice was rising, and he realized he hadn't seen her get upset since she'd come to Alabama. She'd been furious with him then, no doubt, but since then she'd seemed to take everything in stride.

Maybe she was due a freak-out. He felt like freaking out.

They'd been rocking along like everything was fine and like there was no time limit on their relationship, but they'd come face-to-face with that time limit today. When the babies were born, that's when they made the decision. They had to, for all their sakes.

Lacey sniffed and rubbed the tears from under her eyes. "I'm sorry—I'm fine. I want to talk to my dad. I'm just gonna call my dad and tell him that we're having a boy and a girl."

"Of course." Devin put the car in gear and drove out of the parking lot as Lacey placed the call, his head reeling. Emotional whiplash was a real thing. He felt shell-shocked.

He'd been so happy looking at the images of the ultrasound, so overwhelmed with love for those tiny little babies. They had fingers and toes and little faces and they were a part of him and a part of Lacey and, no matter what else happened, they were an amazing gift from God.

And now to realize that Lacey still had so many doubts about their ability to be a family and do what was right… So, she wasn't wrong. They did have a lot of things to settle and they didn't have a lot of time left to do it. But every day they grew closer and knew each other a little better. That had to count for something. Unless it just wasn't enough?

He knew she had family in Oklahoma— he'd met her dad a bunch of times. But hearing her excited voice on the phone talking about the babies terrified him. Before she brought his horse home, she'd planned to have the babies without him. And if they didn't get their relationship figured out soon, she really might leave.

When she did, she'd be taking their babies with her, a thousand miles away from him.

She hung up the phone. "My dad's excited. He's already bought a couple of toddler saddles. I keep telling him he's got a little while before they'll be ready to ride."

Devin guessed maybe it was his turn to be quiet. He didn't know what to say because he knew that, to Lacey, his words had little value. He'd made promises to her that he hadn't kept.

He'd left her. And when she was scared about the future, that was what she remembered. Not all the times they'd come through for each other.

She remembered that he'd left.

Pulling over to the side of the road, he turned to her. "I just want to say right now that if you go back to Oklahoma with our babies…" His voice broke and he had to stop for a minute and get his emotions under control before he could go on. He cleared his throat.

"If you go back to Oklahoma with Prudence and Elmo, I'm going with you. Our babies will have a dad."

She stared at him, her expression unchanging. "Prudence and Elmo. What about Gomer?"

Saying their names, she started to laugh again, which frustrated him. He didn't want to hear laughing.

He wanted to hear that they were in this together.

But when her giggles finally quieted, she put her hand on his. "I don't know what I'm doing. I'm a total mess. When the doctor said we could have the babies in twelve weeks, I freaked out. I'm the girl who always has a five-year plan. There are so many questions about our future and we don't have any answers."

"I know." He brushed the hair away from her face with a gentle hand and wished that he could hold her close and tell her everything would be okay and that she would believe it. "I'm scared, too. But we'll figure it out. Just promise me we'll figure it out together."

She drew in a deep breath, her eyes searching his. She raised her shoulders and let them drop. "Okay. I promise."

He put the car in gear and pulled back onto the road. They still had a lot more questions than they had answers, but for this minute at least, they were committed to figuring out the answers together.

"What in the world?"

Lacey looked up at the sound of Devin's voice. There were cars going every which way in front of their farm stand. People were milling about. One couple was taking a selfie by the old red truck filled with flowers.

Devin pulled over. "I guess we better see what's up."

She got out of the car just as Tanner strode out of the crowd with an empty barrel. He had a wide grin on his face. "I just had to refill the corn and the okra. The zucchini brownies and the cookies are *gone*. Wiped out in the first hour."

"I guess I better make some more."

Devin looked dazed. "How did this happen?"

Tanner shrugged. "All I did was a little ten-minute interview with the local paper. They ran it as a feature today. I had no idea so many people would want to come and check it out."

Jordan Sheehan pulled up next to them with her window rolled down, red hair in a high ponytail on her head. "Did you make these cookies, Lacey?"

Lacey nodded.

"The color's really all natural? Levi can't have anything artificial."

"No artificial anything. Unbleached flour, organic sugar, natural coloring, pure vanilla."

Jordan laughed. "Do you know how hard it is to find a cookie that kid can eat? I'm so excited. I'm going to bring him by after school tomorrow."

Lacey flicked her thumb toward the house. "I'm going to make more cookies."

"Hey, you okay? You look a little shell-shocked."

"Yeah. I'm fine. We just had an ultrasound. It's a boy and a girl."

"Aw! Congrats! It's all feeling pretty real about now, isn't it?" Jordan's eyes were kind and Lacey felt tears well up again.

"So real."

"Let's get some lunch soon and I'll tell you the story of how my oldest joined our family. It's a doozy. Let's just say I can relate to how you're feeling right now."

"Lunch sounds great. Text me the details

and I'll be there." Lacey waved as Jordan pulled away. She looked around for Devin, who seemed to be deep in conversation with someone, so she started for the house. Apparently, she was going to have to make more brownies and cookies.

She smiled to herself. She'd had her doubts about whether the roadside farm stand would work or not, even though it was her idea. She was so thankful that something, at least, was going according to plan.

A frantic moo detoured her to the round pen, where she stopped to rub Nemo's head. He was so soft and so sweet. So loud. Devin was right. He needed a buddy.

In the kitchen, she laid all her ingredients out before starting the food processor to shred the zucchini. She had to admit that slamming the vegetable into the processor and whizzing it to shreds was kind of therapeutic.

So the dream of her future wasn't turning out the way she imagined it and she had feelings about it. Big deal. She was about to be a mother. She didn't have time for unresolved feelings. It was time to get rid of them.

The first zucchini she named anger. She jammed it into the processor and turned it on. *Anger, you are shredded.*

She felt a little silly, but oddly enough it really did help.

Next came fear. She held up the zucchini and shook it. *Fear, you do not have a hold over me.* She shredded it.

Sadness, shredded. Disappointment, shredded.

A tear ran down her cheek. She always tried so hard to find the joy in the moments, to look for the good in things. In people. And usually, she was successful.

In this situation, she was just so out of her depth.

She knew she couldn't do it alone. She could shred all those bad feelings and let them go, but she needed something in their place.

She needed Devin. She needed her family.

And she needed Jesus.

She let her eyes drift closed and took a deep breath, just acknowledging the letting go and the filling up. *I need you, Jesus. I need you to fill all the empty spaces I'm feeling right now.*

"Hey." Devin spoke softly from the doorway. "You good?"

She opened her eyes and smiled. And for the first time in a long time, she really did feel better. "I'm okay. Taking out my feelings on the zucchini. Talking to Jesus about it."

Devin's smile deepened. "I know we talked about this a little bit in the car, but I just wanted to tell you that I understand having doubts and being scared. I'm scared every single day. But that doesn't mean that we can't figure out what to do and be good parents. You're gonna be a great mom."

"Thank you." She lifted her shoulders. "You're right. I am scared. I want to be able to take it all in stride but I can't. I need help."

"I've just gotta tell you, when I looked at those babies on the ultrasound today, I thought my heart was gonna explode. I've never loved anything more than I love them. I'd never do anything to jeopardize their safety."

His words were exactly what she wanted to hear. What she needed to hear. She had no doubt that he meant them, just like she'd meant it when she'd said she was letting go of her fear. Somehow she had to stop being afraid that everything Devin said would disappear like dust in the arena.

Somehow she had to learn to believe him again.

Chapter Twelve

Devin paced in the living room and looked at his watch for the fourteenth time. "We're gonna miss the class if she doesn't hurry. What is she doing in there?"

Tanner looked up from the book he was reading. "Trust me. That's not a question you want to ask."

Devin sucked in a breath, willed himself to be patient and started pacing again. He'd made the reservations for the class two weeks ago when they'd gotten the flier in the mail. She'd agreed to try.

"You're gonna make a hole in the rug with all that tromping back and forth." This time Tanner didn't even look up from his book.

Devin didn't bother answering, just "tromped" back to the opening where the hallway led to the bedroom. "Lacey? We've got to leave or we're going to be late."

The bedroom door opened and she stepped out wearing cropped jeans, a flowy shirt and flip-flops. "You try getting dressed with a beach ball for a belly and then we'll talk."

He wasn't going to give her a chance to back out now. "Makes sense to me. Come on, let's go."

Her steps slowed. "I just want to get something to eat before we leave."

"I packed you a sandwich. It's right here." He scooped up a brown bag that held a sandwich and a bag of chips.

"Oh." She frowned. "I'm going to need…"

"Water?" He picked up an insulated mug. "Right here. Ready to go now?"

"I guess so." Picking up her bag, she followed him out the door.

Devin made the drive to the hospital in a record twenty-four minutes, which he figured was a good practice run for their actual drive to the hospital when Lacey went into labor.

Whipping into the parking lot, he slid into a parking spot. His hand was on the door handle when he looked over at Lacey. "Awesome. We made it with a minute to spare. Let's go…"

The words died on his lips as he looked—really looked—at her. Her hand was clenched around the seat belt, her knuckles white with tension. "Lace? You okay?"

She didn't look at him, just stared straight ahead, giving a quick shake of the head, so small he might've missed it if he hadn't been watching closely.

As her breaths came in quick harsh gasps, he realized she was having a panic attack. Stretching until he could reach the lunch he'd made for her, he dumped the sandwich and chips onto the floor of the truck and handed the empty bag to her. "Breathe into this. Okay?"

Lacey still didn't answer him, but she took the bag and placed it around her lips, closing her eyes.

He'd messed up. He should've believed her when she said she couldn't do this. This wasn't just regular nerves. Her fear was a living, breathing thing, and whether he knew the reason or not, he knew there was one. He put the keys back into the ignition and started the car, pulling out of the parking lot as quickly as he'd pulled in.

For ten minutes or so, he just drove, letting her fear ebb away and her breathing settle.

When she removed the bag and let her head drop against the headrest, he knew she'd gotten through the worst of it.

He spotted an ice cream shop up ahead in a small strip of stores and he pulled up out front. "Let's get some ice cream."

Lacey opened her eyes. "I really just want to go back to the farm."

"So, hear me out and if you still want to go back, I promise I will listen."

She lifted her hands in surrender. "Okay, fine."

"We haven't been on a date. Like, ever, honestly. I want to buy you some ice cream and walk around the park across the street. No agenda, just you and me."

She didn't exactly smile, but her mouth tilted up a smidge. "That actually sounds kind of nice."

"Cool. I could really go for some rocky road. But only if it has actual marshmallows in it. None of that fake marshmallow-ribbon trash."

"I forgot how opinionated you are about ice cream. Maybe I need to rethink this."

"Don't you dare." He grinned and opened the door, grabbing his cane, wishing like crazy he didn't have to.

"I want a double scoop of strawberry."

When he raised an eyebrow, she nudged him with her elbow, laughing when he had to hop to maintain his balance. "You deserved that. Two babies, two scoops. The end."

A few minutes later, they were back on the sidewalk with dripping cones. They didn't talk much, just walked along, eating their ice cream, looking in the windows of the little shops. Devin pointed to a birdhouse in one of the stores. "I bet we could make something like that to sell at the farm stand."

When they passed a jewelry shop, he stopped again, his attention caught by a display of shiny hand-stamped bangles in the window. "Want to go in?"

"I've got to finish my ice cream, but if you want to, go ahead. I'll come in a minute."

He pushed open the door to the store, glancing back to make sure Lacey was still occupied.

"Can I help you?" A woman with long straight blond hair walked toward him.

"Yes. I want one of those bangles with the letters. Like the ones in the window." When she pointed out a display by the register, he picked up the bracelet that had caught his eye. "This one."

He handed her the bracelet and his debit card. A few minutes later, Devin opened the door and stepped outside just as Lacey was finishing up her ice cream and dabbing at her shirt with a napkin. She looked up with a laugh. "I think I got more *onto* my stomach than I got into my stomach. What did you get?"

"You feel like sitting in the park for a minute?"

"Sure." It was so normal—to grab her hand as they crossed the street. He wanted more moments like this when they were just a couple out on a date, when they could relax and just be together.

Devin led Lacey to a bench. Laughter and squeals—and the occasional wail—filtered through from the playground. Parents stood around, some of them still in suits and work clothes, watching as their kids ran out some energy.

"I saw something in the window and thought of you." He handed her the bag, feeling butterflies in his stomach like maybe he'd crossed a line that they weren't ready to cross.

She pulled out the bracelet he'd bought. Her eyes darted to his. She pressed her lips together and once again he worried that he'd made a mistake.

It wasn't anything fancy, just shiny gold-tone brass, but it had the letters *MAMA* stamped on it. She held it in her fingers, just looking at the word. A tear splashed onto the tissue paper it had been wrapped in.

His eyes widened. "It's okay if you don't want to wear it. It was just an impulse buy."

She lunged toward him, wrapping her arms around his neck, their babies between them. With a sigh, he closed his arms around her.

Lacey buried her face in Devin's shoulder. He was just so sweet. In all the anger and angst and absurdity of their situation, she'd forgotten how thoughtful he could be. She sat back, sliding the bracelet on her wrist.

"You're gonna be a great mom, Lacey."

"I love it, Devin." When she looked down at it, she wanted to cry all over again. "I know you don't understand my deal with the hospital."

"No, but I'm not judging. I know you. You're one of the bravest people I know. If you're scared of something, I know you have a good reason."

"It's hard to talk about. I've—I've never told anyone."

"You can tell me when you're ready, Lacey. It doesn't have to be now."

"I know. And that you trust me without knowing the story just makes me want to tell you more." She smiled, but her stomach turned with anxiety. "Did you know I broke my arm when I was five? The day I turned five, actually."

He shook his head and she went on. "My parents had gotten me roller skates for my birthday. They gave them to me that morning before my dad went out to work on the ranch. I begged my mom all day to let me try them out, but she wanted to wait until my dad got back. She said her back was hurting."

"That seems like it would be hard for a five-year-old to understand."

"Oh, it was. I was so upset. I begged and cried and pleaded. Finally, she told me if I could get them on, I could go out to the garage and skate out there."

Devin's arm slid around her shoulders. "I don't like where this story is going."

He had no idea. Really no idea.

In her mind, she could see her feet with the shiny white skates and the tangled-up laces.

Her five-year-old self had imagined that she would skim across the floor like one of the ice skaters she'd watched on TV. "You know how stubborn I am?"

He nodded. "I'm acquainted with that side of you."

"I didn't know how to tie shoes but I smushed them around and wadded them up and convinced myself that it was just as good as being tied. And when I pushed off the step, thinking I was going to glide on my new skates, what really happened is that the laces got tangled around the wheel and I went down hard on the concrete floor. I broke my arm in two places. It was terrible."

She looked up to find his eyes, filled with distress and concern, on hers.

"My mom was really mad. It was what she'd been warning me about all day, but she took me to the emergency room and waited with me until they put me in a room." She swallowed hard, the ache in her throat making it hard to talk. "By that time, I was in shock and I was scared. I begged her to stay with me, but she said she wanted some coffee. She told me she was going to the cafeteria and… She left."

"You must have been terrified. You were so little."

She ran her fingers across the letters that spelled *mama* on her bracelet. "That was the last time I saw my mom."

"What?" His eyes went wide with shock.

With a little shrug, she told him the rest of it before she could chicken out. "I waited for hours but she never came back. They wouldn't fix my arm without someone there to sign the papers. It seemed like forever before they finally got my dad on the phone."

"That's a horrible thing to do to a little kid." He shook his head. "I'm so sorry, Lacey."

His words loosened something for that little five-year-old who had been so scared and sad. "I thought it was my fault because I wouldn't leave her alone about the skates. Now I know there was nothing I could have done to stop her. If it hadn't been the skates, it would've been something else."

"It was *not* your fault." He said it so vehemently that she had to laugh a little.

"I don't know where she is now. My dad got divorce papers in the mail a few months later. Sometimes I would look for her face in the stands when I was racing. It's silly. I don't really even remember what she looked like."

"It's not silly. She was your mom and she should've been there. That's on her."

"I do know that much." She shrugged. "And I know rationally that I shouldn't be afraid of the hospital. I've tried so many times to just walk through that door without a thought, but every time I freeze up. Or worse, have a panic attack like I did tonight."

"I'm so sorry I didn't know. I wouldn't have pressured you to take that ridiculous class."

"I want to take the class. That's the part that makes me so frustrated."

"You do?" He went quiet for a minute, watching as the parents on the playground called their kids to go. The sun was sinking in the sky and, even on a summer evening, it was time for them to head home for baths and bedtime. "What if we try again? No pressure, we'll just see how far we get."

She had her doubts, but he seemed so hopeful. "Maybe."

"I'll set it up. We'll try to go and if we don't, we don't. No big thing. At least we'll be together. Deal?"

She studied his face with a million thoughts running through her mind, mostly about how it was a terrible idea to put herself through that over and over again. But she had to try because as much as she'd like to imagine that the babies would just appear when the time came, the fact was she would be giving birth in a hospital. She had to face it at some point.

She sighed, shaking her head. "Deal."

They stood up together. Devin pulled her in for a sideways hug. "I'm so sorry I left you in Vegas. It must have felt like being abandoned all over again."

"Yeah, it did, kind of. It brought up a lot of feelings I thought I'd gotten over."

"I don't deserve a second chance."

She shook her head. "Nope. But our babies deserved a chance at a dad. And maybe I wasn't ready to give up on us, either. I don't know what's going to happen, Devin. I do know that I'm glad I've had the chance to get to know you again."

As they turned back toward the car, she slid her fingers into his. "How do *you* feel? I don't want to pry, but I'm curious. Does being sober feel like a relief? Is it stressful? Do you ever stop thinking about it?"

They walked along in silence for a few minutes, and the sounds around them soaked into her consciousness. Cars whizzed by. Bells jingled as people entered the little shops. Live music filtered in from a nearby restaurant.

But it was his hand clasping hers that felt real and present.

"It's hard to put in words, but to answer your question, being sober is a relief. Having my addiction out in the open is a relief. The stressful part—for me anyway, but it's probably different for everyone—is that I feel like I have so much to make up for. I broke trust with you and with my family. With my corporate sponsors. And some of that I'll never get back."

"Do you ever stop thinking about it?"

"My ankle reminds me. But every once in a while I forget. I go to meetings because I need to be reminded that I'm an addict and because being with other people who continue to be sober is helpful."

"Do you think you'll ever do drugs or drink again?" It was a loaded question, and one she desperately needed an answer to.

He was quiet. "I don't think so. But I can only be responsible for these twenty-four hours right now. I know I'm not going to drink or take painkillers today. I'll go to a meeting later tonight because it helps me stay sober tomorrow. Does that seem weird?"

"A little bit, but only because I haven't experienced it."

They got to the car and he beeped the locks open, but he didn't say anything else. They drove home in silence. She wasn't sure where his mind was, but she knew her mind was spinning with all the things they'd talked about tonight.

She was almost grateful for her panic attack because she felt like Devin had opened up to her in a way he never had before.

When they pulled in the driveway at the house, he put the truck in Park but he didn't turn it off or get out. The light from the porch glinted off her bracelet. She cleared her throat. "You said I'm brave, Devin, but I need you to know that I think you're the brave one. You live with pain every day, and despite that, you're doing what it takes to be the person your family needs you to be. I respect that. I'm not impressed by how hot you are or how long you can stick on a bucking bronc. I'm not impressed by your gold buckle. I am impressed by how you're trying to do what's best for you and your family."

His breath was shaky. He looked away, but he reached for her hand again. "I don't think I'm worthy of your respect, Lacey. I've got my demons to face down, just like you."

She nodded. "You told me I didn't have to face mine alone. Well, neither do you."

The surprising thing was, she meant it. She'd been thinking of his battle with addiction as something he had to conquer alone. But this wasn't some goal he'd set for himself, like sticking to the saddle longer, or pushing himself in the ring just a little further. This was real-life important.

That didn't mean that she'd forgotten what he did or that everything was okay between them forever. But he'd been there beside her today as she'd fought her battle.

And she could be beside him as he fought his.

Chapter Thirteen

Lacey stumbled into the kitchen for her daily cup of coffee. It was getting difficult for her to sleep between the twins deciding that her sleep time was their playtime and the random contractions she assumed were Braxton Hicks.

She'd heard the guys as they got up for breakfast, but she stayed in her room. After sharing her childhood trauma with Devin last night, she felt a little tender. A little crowded, almost—not by Devin, but by her overly large emotions. *Thanks, pregnancy.*

When Tanner and Devin had left to do their chores, she'd drifted back to sleep and slept way longer than she intended. She had lots to bake today. But coffee came first.

After dumping enough cream in the left-over coffee to make it palatable, she slid her feet into flip-flops and walked out the front door onto the porch. The ceiling fans were on, creating a breeze, which was good because even at 10:00 a.m., the temperature was already soaring.

Nemo was standing at the edge of the ring facing the pasture, mooing for all he was worth. Then she realized Devin was up on Dolly, working her in the field as Nemo bellowed. He could get about halfway across the field toward the loud little calf before the horse would slow down. Each time Devin would gently guide her back toward the round pen.

He was striking on horseback, always had been. It was no wonder she'd had such a crush on him from the first time he'd stepped into the arena. But really, she knew. He was meant for her. In so many ways, he was meant for her. There was a mountain range of problems between them, but she hoped and prayed they were steadily making progress through them.

Lacey walked, mug in hand, across the driveway to lean on the fence, so she could see Devin at work. He was so patient and so calm with Dolly. From her new vantage point, she realized that Sadie was in the pasture, too. When Dolly would start to shy, Devin would give Sadie a command and she would take the lead, showing Dolly that there was nothing to fear ahead.

It was beautiful to watch the rapport between the animals and Devin. He was in his element. Almost as if he'd heard her thoughts, he glanced up, smiling when he saw her standing by the fence. She wondered if he was thinking of last night, too. Her cheeks heated again and she looked down, suddenly feeling shy.

Tires crunched on the gravel driveway behind her. She turned around as Garrett got out of his SUV, slammed the door and waved. "Hey, it looks like there's a good crowd at the farm stand today. You hired a teenager to work it?"

"When she can. We check in on things, replacing the produce and baked goods when we have them."

"I want to get some of those zucchini brownies before I go."

"Sure." Lacey heard a noise from the back of Garrett's SUV. "What was that? Is there an animal in there?"

Garrett's face went ruddy. "Uh, yeah. I did some legal work for a farmer I know. He offered to pay me with a couple of kids he was planning to bottle raise."

Her mouth dropped open. "Oh… Tanner's gonna kill you."

"Yeah, I know." Garrett laughed, but he walked over to the SUV and opened the back, pulling out a big dog crate and placing it on the ground. When he opened it up, two of the tiniest goats she'd ever seen bounded out. They tilted their heads and let out the sweetest little bleats.

Fuzzy and white with black markings and little black hooves, they were adorable. One of them kind of toddled over to her and pulled on the leg of her pants with his soft goat lips. If she'd been able to get back up, she would've dropped to her knees immediately to cuddle him.

"Oh, Garrett. They're so cute."

"Right? How could I refuse?"

From the fence, Devin said, "You say no. That's how."

"You're one to talk while you're riding a horse someone gave you." Garrett grinned. "Tanner'll get over it. He's just a little slow to adjust to change."

"They're really cute. I bet Nemo will like having friends." Lacey leaned over and scratched the littlest one on the head. "What are you naming them?"

"Thelma and Louise."

"Perfect." She laughed. "I hope they don't get in quite that much trouble."

Dolly was snacking on some grass while Devin chatted, and Sadie, recognizing a chance to nap, came under the fence to lie down at Lacey's feet.

"We're going to have to make a pen in part of the north pasture for these guys. The round pen is fine while they're bottle-feeding, but they're going to need grass soon." Devin patted Dolly's neck.

His brother nodded. "I'll look at my calendar for next week and see when I can do it."

"And you're going to drive out here four times a day to feed them?" Devin tightened up on the reins as one of the little goats got closer to Dolly. The horse shied away, but she acted more curious than afraid. "She's doing better. Did you see that?"

"She's doing great." Lacey laughed as one of the goat babies tried to jump on Sadie's back and fell off. "I would help feed if I could."

Garrett shoved his hands in his jeans pockets. "I thought maybe I'd stay in the cabin by the creek for a few weeks until they're settled in and can go longer between bottles."

Devin nodded slowly. "Works for me. The place is a dump, though."

"It needs some maintenance, so it'll be a good time for me to do it after work. We can't afford to let the roof fall in."

"All right, sounds fine to me, but you have to tell Tanner." Devin looked toward the house. "Confound it, Garrett, they're eating my daisies."

Garrett ran for the house as Lacey laughed. "Those goats are going to give him a run for his money. He has no idea."

Devin shook his head. "No idea."

Walking back with one goat under each arm, his tie flapping over his shoulder, Garrett said, "I don't know what to do with them."

"Put them in the round pen with Nemo. We've been leaving the door open to the barn." Devin clucked to Dolly. "We're going around a few more times and then I'm putting her in the pasture next to Reggie for the rest of the day."

As Devin rode away, Lacey turned to Garrett. "Are the bottles in the trunk? I'll get today's ready for you, if you want me to."

"That would be so awesome, Lacey. There's

a shopping bag with a bunch of stuff in the back of the SUV."

"I'll get them. You get Thelma and Louise settled with Nemo. You might want to check the hay in the open stall and make sure it's fresh." She walked around to the back of the SUV and retrieved the bag of goat supplies. There were two small bottles and a gallon container of goat's milk that the farmer must've given Garrett.

She hated to tell him, but that wasn't going to go very far. He was going to have to figure out what to feed these guys and fast.

They had babies coming out their ears here at Triple Creek Ranch. Prudence—or Elmo—gave her a big kick in the ribs as an exclamation point to her thought. She rubbed her belly. "Hey, watch it, there, little one."

There was another kick in response. Lacey chuckled. "I think you get that behavior from your dad."

She dumped the calf bottles and the goat bottles into the sink to wash them out and put some water on to boil to make Nemo's formula.

Her eye caught on the flier from the hospital for the Magnificent Multiples class. It was only a couple of weeks before she'd promised to try again.

This time, at least, she knew what she was up against and Devin was aware of her fears. It was for the babies.

This time she would handle it.

Devin flipped over in bed and kicked the covers off. The clock said 3:24 and he hadn't been to sleep yet. His ankle was aching from his time up on Dolly today, the muscles in his leg spasming from trying to compensate.

He stared at the ceiling for another minute before deciding to get up and try some chamomile tea. Sometimes it would relax his muscles enough to sleep.

Rolling out of bed, he stumbled into the kitchen, stopping short when he saw Lacey sitting at the kitchen table, a tray of cookies in front of her and a bag of frosting in her hand. "Hey, what are you doing up? It's three in the morning."

She jumped and frosting squirted out of the bag in a long stream. "You scared me! Give a girl some warning next time you sneak up on her in the middle of the night."

"Sorry." He limped to the stove, slid the

kettle onto the burner and started it up. "I'm making some chamomile tea. Want some?"

"Sure." She filled in the frosting on a cookie that looked like a flip-flop and laid down her piping bag. "So why are you awake?"

"Ankle hurting. You?"

"Couldn't get comfortable with this big ole belly. And apparently, the twins find my sleeping time to be the ideal playtime. It's like they're doing karate in there."

"Don't take this the wrong way, but is it weird? It seems like it would be."

"Yeah, it's kind of weird when you think about four arms and four legs and two heads." She laughed. "I just freaked myself out a little bit. I'm sorry you're hurting."

"It's okay." He poured the steaming water over the tea bags he'd placed in the mugs. "I've learned to make peace with it, for the most part."

"What do you mean?" She slid a cookie over to him.

"You asked me if I thought I'd ever drink or take pills again. I know I had the reputation of always being up for a party. But for me, the drinking and the drugs weren't about the partying. Or really even about the high.

It was about…stopping the pain." He broke the cookie in half and took a bite.

"Oh, Devin. And you're still dealing with the pain."

"Yes." He very carefully dunked the tea bag in his mug. It was easier to talk when he wasn't looking at her. He was so much more comfortable making her laugh than he was with serious conversations. "I can frame it differently now, though."

She picked the piping bag back up and began the process of frosting another cookie, but her brow furrowed. She still didn't know what he meant.

"I try to remember something I learned in therapy." He took a sip of his tea. It was too hot and he burned his mouth. He set the cup down. "The pain in my body reminds me that I'm alive. If I dull the pain with drugs or alcohol, I dull everything else too…joy and laughter, even the ability to make a decision that's both sorrowful and sweet."

Her eyes on the cookie in front of her, she asked the question he always dreaded to answer. "Was it only physical pain you were trying to dull?"

Devin looked away. He didn't want to talk about his parents. It was one thing to share memories about his mom or dad, but talking about how he felt about their dying was different. His feelings about his parents' death were complicated. A toxic mix of sadness and guilt and grief.

"My parents' death…" His voice thickened and he stopped to clear his throat. "It's been so long. I don't understand why it's so hard to talk about. Or why it affects how I live my life now. Why it still…hurts so much."

"You don't have to talk about it, Devin. Of all people, I understand that."

But he had a choice to make. Either he was all in with Lacey or he wasn't. Either she knew everything about him or he'd always wonder if things would've been different.

Their pasts had such an effect on their present—who they were and the decisions they made. That was never clearer than when he'd tried to get Lacey to go into the hospital for that class.

In the wee hours of the morning, the kitchen felt cozy, a small cone of light in a dark, silent house. It felt safe, as if they were the only two people awake in the world right now. The words came without his bidding. "I was in middle school, at football practice. I was supposed to get a ride home from practice with my friend Sam, but I messed around and by the time I realized I needed to leave, Sam's mom had already come and gone. I, um, borrowed the coach's phone to call my mom. My parents had already passed the school on their way home from picking Tanner's wife and baby up from the airport, but she said they would come and get me. I heard my mom tell my dad they needed to turn around. My dad was grumbling, but he did it. A few seconds later, I heard the crash."

Tears were pooling in her eyes when he looked up. She blinked and twin tears streaked her cheeks. "Oh, Devin."

He swallowed over the ache in his throat. The next part was the hardest to get through. "I screamed into the phone. Begged my mom to answer me. For a few minutes, I heard crying and then just…nothing. We found out later that the man who hit them had been distracted by a bird hitting his windshield. He hit them broadside as they turned back onto the road. His air bags worked. He survived. Tanner's baby, my nephew, was the only one alive when they pulled them out of the car. He died the next day."

She didn't say anything. He didn't expect her to. What could you say to a story like that?

He stared into the amber tea, his eyes following a lone bubble on the surface until it popped. And he said the words that had haunted his mind since the day of the accident. The real reason he'd pushed himself so hard. The real reason he'd nearly destroyed himself. The pain didn't come from his ruined ankle.

The pain came from inside him. "It was my fault."

Her head jerked up. "No. Devin, *no*. It wasn't your fault. You didn't cause the accident."

"If I'd just done what my mom told me to do, I'd have been home waiting when they got there. I've relived that afternoon a million times. More. If I'd just gotten in the car with Sam, they'd be alive right now. All of them."

"You don't know that." She reached across the table to touch him and he grabbed her hand like a lifeline. "Devin, you don't know that. They could've stopped to let a dog pass in front of them, or gotten held up in a traffic jam, or had to stop to pick up milk. Anything could've been the variable that had them right there at that exact moment."

He shook his head. "Any of those things could have happened but I know I was the reason they were turning around to come back to the school. I have to live with that."

"Okay. I understand that. I believe it was an accident but I understand you feeling the way you do." Her eyes were huge in her face, and Devin suddenly felt like he should be comforting her instead of the other way around.

With a sigh, he admitted the truth that he was finally facing about his addiction. "I was reckless and stupid, trying to numb the pain with drugs and alcohol and adrenaline. And I was too selfish to see that I wasn't just hurting myself. I was hurting you. Tanner and Garrett. And my mom wouldn't want me to live my life like that. She'd want me to take care of my brothers. And she'd want me to be happy."

She swiped at the tears on her cheeks, and the knowledge slammed him in the gut. He loved her so much.

He'd known it forever. He just didn't think he was worthy of love in return. And now things were so complicated between them... He just had to pray that God could work things out where Devin couldn't.

He reached over and gently rubbed a tear away with his thumb. "That morning in Vegas, I didn't know we'd gotten married, but I knew I needed to get help. Because hurting you was the last thing I wanted to do."

Lacey scrubbed her hands over her face. "How did we manage to mess things up so badly?"

"I seem to have a talent for it." He picked up his mug and drained the rest of his ice-cold tea. "Are you ready to get back to bed yet?"

"I'm gonna finish these cookies before I go back so you can take them out to the stand in the morning. I'm not sleepy and the babies are still in the mood to rumble, apparently."

"I'll head up, then." He grabbed his cane and walked to the door before he stopped. "I just want to say one thing before I go. This thing between us, it's not about responsibility to me."

Lacey pushed to her feet and walked over to him, stopping about a foot away, her eyes locked on his.

He shifted his weight. "I know I don't deserve—"

She grabbed his shirt, dragged him to her and kissed him. He sighed. Finally.

Finally.

His arms closed around her, the sweetness of sugar and vanilla permeating his senses.

She took a step back, her cheeks a little

rosy. "It's not about responsibility for me, either. I just wanted to make that clear."

Looking down, he laughed. "Okay, then. I'll see you in the morning."

"See you in the morning."

Chapter Fourteen

Lacey closed her eyes as Devin pulled into the parking lot at the hospital. They were trying an afternoon class this time, and despite his running description of every bronc he'd ever gotten thrown off and her own determination to breathe through her anxiety, she wasn't sure she could get through it.

"Lacey?"

"I've survived way worse than a class in a hospital. I can do this." He'd barely pulled into the parking space when she opened the door to the car and slid out.

"Lacey…"

He sounded unsure, and she glanced back at him. "It's only for an hour."

The words were firm in her mind but her voice sounded weak and breathy to her ears.

She focused on the door to the hospital. *It's like any other door.* She took one step. Two. And despite all her efforts, she felt it as her brain took over and her fight-or-flight response kicked in.

Heart rate jacked. Breathing shallow. Muscles tensing. Vision narrowing.

She faltered to a stop, her body swaying as her vision swam.

Devin's arm, strong and steady, moved around her waist, bolstering her, turning her back toward the car. "Come on. We're leaving. We can try again in two weeks."

He opened the door to the truck and she slid in, her body feeling boneless. Why was this so hard? She knew it was irrational. She just didn't know how to fight it.

"I'm sorry," she whispered when he got in on the other side and cranked the truck up with a roar.

"No worries, babe. We'll try again. Right now, I say we go shopping."

"Shopping?"

"Yep. I got my last check from my corporate sponsor about a week ago and I tucked it away for baby stuff."

"I don't know, Devin…" She knew they had to shop for all the things they needed.

And she wasn't in denial that they were about to have twins. It was that shopping for all the stuff together seemed a lot like planning for her to be here after the babies were born.

It was intimate, too, a thing couples did together. The last thing she wanted was an awkward hour in a baby store with Devin, but considering the kiss she laid on him last night, she should probably get over that. Her cheeks heated as she thought about it now.

Yeah, she passed awkward a long time ago.

Devin kept driving. "It'll be fun. We can get a big *P* to go over Prudence's bed and a big *E* to go over Elmo's."

Lacey shot him a look. "That was a *joke*."

Pulling into the parking lot at a store called Heaven Sent, Devin said, "When the owners named their store, do you think they were thinking about the babies being 'Heaven sent' or were they thinking about all the new parents who were going to spend all their money here?"

"The second one, for sure. I definitely think they're most interested in your credit card." She unbuckled and got out of the car. When he held the door open for her, she walked in and immediately melted. Pale pastels, luxurious textures. Precious prints. Everything seemed so soft and sweet. So perfect for tiny fragile humans.

Devin walked past her with a cart, stopped where the aisle turned and looked back. "You coming?"

She wanted to say yes. She wanted to dive right into the fun of picking out all the things for the twins. But she stopped herself. Staying in Alabama had been about giving herself time to come to a decision.

This was a big step.

She'd trusted Devin in Vegas and he'd left her. Now it wasn't even as much about trusting him as trusting her own judgment. She'd been so wrong about him before. She was falling for him again, but what if she was wrong now?

This shopping trip, as wonderful as the idea was, felt like losing her power to make the best decision, the safest decision, for her and the babies.

She shook her head. "Devin, I'm not sure if this is a good idea. You've been trying so hard. And I...really appreciate that. But it's only been a few months. What if you buy a ton of stuff and I don't...it doesn't work out for us?"

"Do you think it's not going to work out for us?"

She didn't answer him. "Why don't we just get one of those portable crib things? I saw one online that had twin bassinets in the top."

His face hardened into stubborn lines. "It's important to me that the babies have actual cribs and an actual nursery. I know we still have decisions to make, but I don't want them to feel like they're negotiable in my life."

"Where are we even going to put them? There's no room for baby beds in the master bedroom."

"I have some thoughts on that. My mom's sitting room is right next to the master bedroom where you're sleeping. No one has used it since… Well, no one has used it. I thought we could make that the nursery."

The fact that he'd been thinking about where the babies would sleep and planning this shopping trip was a good sign. But at the same time, the fact that he'd made some big decisions without talking them over with her made her uncomfortable.

Devin dug a piece of paper out of his pocket. "I made a list. Want to start with the cribs? Come on, this will be fun. Do we need two?"

Reluctantly, Lacey followed him across the

store. "I guess? Or maybe we could just get one. I think sometimes people let twins share until they get a little bit bigger."

She wandered into one of the mock-up nurseries, sliding her finger along the soft white wood railing on one of the cribs. "I like this one."

"I like it, too. It's low to the ground and I think it's small enough to fit two in that sitting room. How about the gray ones?"

She scowled, finding herself annoyed that he wanted to choose the color of the crib. "White would go with everything. We can leave the walls white, too, and use different colors for their bedding."

"Okay, white's kind of predictable, but they're babies. I don't think they'll care." He picked up two of the tags from the display attached to the rail, looked at his list and laughed. "We have so much stuff on this list."

They walked through the store, Devin pushing the cart, Lacey lagging behind. She'd come to Alabama for a divorce, and instead she'd gotten options. But now? With every baby item he tossed into the cart, it felt like her options were getting more and more limited. Like she was racing closer to a life with Devin and their babies at Triple Creek. Preparing for the twins to arrive and planning a nursery was another set of roots growing deep, anchoring her to Red Hill Springs.

A faint echo of the panic she'd felt at the hospital began in her chest. She stopped walking, took some deep breaths and tried to think logically. Her stress made sense. She'd had no control over her life when her mother decided to abandon her. No control when Devin had left her in Vegas.

In coming to Red Hill Springs to confront Devin, she'd taken the reins back for herself—or so she thought.

Now she wasn't so sure.

She'd learned so much about him since coming here. But the sting—no, that word didn't begin to touch how she'd felt that night—the *devastation* of being left by Devin on their wedding night was still there. Even worse was the realization that she hadn't known him at all—she'd only thought she had.

Things were different now. With every confidence offered, every late-night secret shared, they grew closer to a real relationship, an honest one. But she was a long way from being able to trust him with her life, with the babies' lives. Trusting his sweet-talking promises hadn't gotten her anywhere before but married, pregnant and alone.

"How about stars for the bedding? Blue for P and yellow for E?" His voice broke into her thoughts. She looked up to see Devin holding up two packages of crib sheets.

She took another deep breath and tried to concentrate. "I love the colors. I was planning to color-code the babies. If you like blue and yellow, we could use those colors for everything."

"It's a brilliant idea. Let's go pick out bottles."

Within an hour, they had a cart full. Two sets of everything: bottles, pacifiers, swaddling blankets, bedding, baby swings and bouncy seats. And Devin had arranged for the cribs and a rocker to be delivered the next day.

She consulted his list. "Okay, the only thing left here is a baby monitor and infant car seats. We have to decide if we want a separate stroller or a whole-system thingy."

Devin stopped the cart. "I saw a video monitor back there with the sound machines, so we can get that. But maybe we need to do a little more research on the car seats."

"We have time, but that's one thing we really do need. We won't be able to leave the hospital without them."

"Noted. We'll get the car seats as soon as possible. I'm going to check out. Why don't you go to the truck so you can get off your feet?"

He was directing her without consulting her again, but her lower back and hips ached from the strain of two babies. "Fine. I'm exhausted. And starving."

After checking out, Devin loaded everything into the back of his truck and slid into the seat beside her. "Whew. I'm tired. How about a burger?"

She *did* want a burger. But she also really, really wanted to be the one to make the decision, even if it was only what they had for dinner. "I want pizza. And I'm ready to go back to the house."

"Okay, pizza sounds good. Pepperoni?"

"Cheese."

"Cheese it is."

She watched him as he carefully backed out of the parking spot. She knew he was working hard to stay sober, working hard at the farm and just in general trying to do right by the people he cared about.

He'd been happy and excited today in the

baby store, patient and kind with her at the hospital. She could see him as a dad one day, showing their kids how to bottle-feed a calf or patiently guide a horse.

They'd been making slow and steady progress, but with the kiss last night and the whirlwind shopping trip today, things suddenly felt like they were out of her control. A big reminder that she was living in Devin's world.

Back at the ranch, Devin grabbed the still-warm box of pizza they'd picked up in town. "We can unload all the stuff later if you want to eat first."

"That would be great." Lacey didn't look at him, just made her way to the porch with Sadie dancing a welcome around her legs. She dropped into a chair. "I'm so tired."

He slid the box onto the table between them and flipped the lid open. She grabbed a piece and bit into it with a sigh.

"I'm sorry it was such a long afternoon," he said, "but I'm glad we got some stuff for the babies. I guess we'll need to get some baby clothes next." He glanced at her as he took his first bite, trying to read her face. He knew something wasn't right. He just couldn't put his finger on what. Or why. In the few months Lacey had been in Red Hill Springs, they had carefully stayed away from making any plans for the future, but he was ready to take some cautious steps forward. Unfortunately, he wasn't sure Lacey had the same feeling.

She'd gone along with his plan for the afternoon but she hadn't seemed very happy about it. Not unhappy, exactly, just not committed to the idea of building a nursery.

But he'd meant what he said to her in the store. He didn't want to feel like the babies were visiting. He didn't want her to feel that way, either. The thought struck him. *Oh*.

Maybe that was part of the problem. The room that was Lacey's was a room his mother had decorated. It didn't have anything of Lacey in it. For as much as Lacey had made this old farmhouse feel like a home again for him, he didn't think she'd say the same.

It was something to think about. He picked up another slice just as Lacey finished her second piece.

She leaned back in the chair. "I want another piece but there's no room."

"Oh, man. That's a complication of pregnancy I never considered." Devin finished up the crust on his, closed the lid and picked up the box. "I'll take this inside and stick it in the fridge so you'll have some later if you get hungry."

When he came back out with his guitar, she was sitting on the porch steps, her legs stretched out in front of her. He sat down on the step beside her and started picking a little tune.

The stars shone bright and clear out here in the country, away from city lights. Devin could hear the animals shuffling in the barn, the cows in the pasture down the dirt road. The night was peaceful and he prayed that he could claim that peace for himself.

He prayed that Lacey would feel it, too, that she would know how much he cared about her. That was what the shopping trip was about today. As much as he wanted things to be settled, he knew she was still scared. He'd left her and she was afraid if she trusted him again that he would break her heart. But how did you prove that something *wouldn't* happen in the future?

All he could do was show her every day that he had grown. That his priorities had changed. Taking a risk with his life seemed to come naturally to him. Taking a risk with his heart, a lot less so, but he was willing to try.

He looked down at his fingers on the guitar and began, hesitantly, to play a tune he'd written a few weeks ago. He looked at Lacey and sang, *"I'll be your sunshine when it rains. You'll be my antidote to pain. I'll be your sweater when you get cold. You'll be my soul mate when I grow old."*

With her eyes full of some unnamed emotion, she watched his fingers on the strings. He had no idea what she was thinking, but he sang the chorus straight to her. *"We may be mismatched like your cowgirl socks, but I'm yours for life, Lacey, you're my rock."*

He smiled as the words repeated. *"Bah-bah-duh, may be mismatched like your cowgirl socks, but I'm yours for life, Lacey, you're my rock."*

As his fingers plucked the last couple of chords, he chuckled into the self-conscious silence that followed. He waited for Lacey to respond with a joke like she so often did, and when she didn't, he supplied one himself. "I don't think I'm going to have a career writing music."

A tear slid down her cheek. Lacey looked away from him as she whispered, "I don't want to love you again."

At her words, his fingers paused on the

strings, but he picked it up again. "I know. It's okay."

"I'm sorry I was so out of sorts today. I wish I could blame pregnancy hormones, but I'm pretty sure it's just me. I love all the stuff we picked out. And I love the song." She let her head drop in her hands. The words that followed were halting, her voice husky with pent-up emotion. "Everything feels like it's spinning out of control."

Devin laid his guitar to the side and put his arm around her. He'd caused her pain and he couldn't fix it. He didn't know how. So, he just sat there with her while she cried.

After a few minutes, he said, "I remember the first time I saw you. I think you might've been eighteen."

"Nineteen," she corrected without looking up.

"You swaggered into the barn with your big brown eyes and your cowboy hat. You had on jeans and boots and a shirt that said Get Up, Show Up, Never Give Up. I walked over to talk to you and you said—"

"Excuse me, I don't have time for you to hit on me. I'm taking care of my horse right now." She interrupted him with the words she'd said when she first met him six years ago, and her eyes met his. "I was such a jerk."

He laughed. "I think my heart fell right out of my chest onto the floor of the barn. Even though you blew me off, it was the beginning of our friendship. And even though it may not feel like it right now, this is a different kind of beginning, Lace. We're still finding our way, but we're gonna be okay."

He didn't know for sure that what he said was true. Her fears were big and they were justified.

Get up, show up, never give up.

He could beg her to stay, but in the end, the choice was hers. It had always been hers.

Chapter Fifteen

Devin opened the door to the future nursery. It was a light and bright room, which had been his mom's hiding place when the testosterone in her household got to be a bit too much. No leather or random sports equipment in this room... The space had been filled with flowers and ruffles and girly-scented candles.

Garrett let out a low whistle. "I haven't been in here in years. It looks exactly the same, like she should be sitting on the couch and yelling at us for interrupting her prayer time."

"I know, right?" Devin and his brothers hadn't been allowed in there without knocking. Even then, admittance was dicey. Being the youngest, he remembered often sitting on the floor with a basket of crayons and a coloring book until he started school.

Mom had used the room for her quiet time. He had so many memories of opening the door to find her leaned over her Bible, tracing the words with her finger, or listening to a sermon while she crocheted.

None of them had any reason to go into her sitting room since the accident. It had been dusted from time to time, but otherwise it had remained exactly the same, none of them wanting to be the one to clean out their mother's stuff. It was still hard, even with so much distance.

But it was time. The last thing Mom would've wanted would be for this room to sit unused. She'd taken so much pleasure in it.

"Mom would be happy that we're doing this." Garrett picked up a stack of magazines from a decade ago and tossed them into a trash bag. "She'd be mad that we let it go so long."

Devin nodded. "I can just hear her now. *You boys—*"

"*—I shouldn't have to ask you to do something that clearly needs doing.*" Garrett completed the sentence they'd heard their mother say at least a thousand times. "She could really be bossy."

With a laugh, Devin grabbed a garbage bag and started shoving the throw pillows from the couch in there. "She really could, but then, she had three rowdy boys that would just as soon wrestle as listen."

Tanner stuck his head in the door. "I wasn't rowdy."

Garrett rolled his eyes. "*Pffffft.* I beg to differ. You just didn't get caught as often."

"I've got a few minutes if you want me to start on the closet."

Devin grimaced. "It pains me to say this, but we could use your help with the furniture. We're planning to load up the back of the truck and take it all over to the cabin."

With Garrett and Tanner hefting the couch, Devin grabbed the cushions he could carry and followed them outside to toss them in with the sofa.

Lacey came out the front door right after him with the last two cushions. "It looks so much bigger in there without the couch. Are you moving the rest of the furniture, too?"

"Yes, except for the dresser that Mom used as a TV stand. I thought we could wait on that and you can decide if you want it in there or not. Do you think anything else should stay?" He wasn't going to stop trying to move them forward, even if they were taking baby steps. But after yesterday's conversation with Lacey about how out of control she felt, he hoped maybe it would help if she were making the decisions.

"Y'all should go ahead and move the furniture. I'm headed over to Jordan's for lunch. But when I come back, we can take a look and talk about the rest of it?"

"Sounds good." Devin stumbled backward as his brother nailed him with a big black bag.

Garrett laughed as he bounded down the stairs. "They're throw pillows, get it?"

"Oh, I get it." Devin grinned and slowly reached into the bag.

Lacey made a T with her hands. "Time out, children. Wait till the pregnant lady is out of the way." To Devin she said, "I'll see you later."

Devin watched as she got into the truck and started it up. Surprisingly, he wasn't too disheartened by their conversation the night before. Instead, he actually felt like they were getting somewhere. She cared about him, and that wasn't any baby step, either, even if she was unhappy about it.

A throw pillow drilled him in the side of the head. "Stop mooning and let's get this done."

Devin whirled around to see Garrett doubled over. "Who's mooning?"

Tanner shook his head. "You are. Most definitely. Mooning."

Not even taking offense because it was true, Devin smiled. "Come on, let's get this furniture to the cabin. I've got a nursery to clean up."

Lacey passed the driveway to Jordan's house twice before she finally saw the teensy-weensy sign that said Sheehan beside a small opening in the trees. She pulled up to a home that looked like it had been built last century and lovingly restored.

She could hear a baby crying from inside the house when she stepped onto the porch. She knocked on the door and waited. With her hand raised to knock again, she heard footsteps.

Jordan opened the door, a very small baby in her arms. Essie, whom Lacey had held the day at Red Hill Farm, was on a blanket on the floor screaming her head off. Jordan raised her voice. "Hey, come on in. Sorry about the noise. Everyone was in a great mood until about five minutes ago when Amos had a poopy diaper at the same time Essie decided she was ready for a nap."

She held the tiny baby out to Lacey. "You mind?"

"Oh. Um. Okay." Lacey took the baby from Jordan, who immediately went to pick Essie up from the floor. "Who is this again?"

Jordan laughed as she settled in an oversize rocker-recliner with Essie, tossed a muslin blanket over her shoulder and began to feed her. "My sister and her husband are Amos's foster parents, but on the day he was supposed to come home from the hospital, two of the other kids came down with strep throat. Amos was a preemie, and since Ash and I are still licensed to foster, we said he could stay here with us until they've been clear for a few days."

"That makes sense. I think." As she eased onto the love seat, Lacey looked down at Amos snuggling in her arms. He blinked up at her with eyes so dark blue they were almost black. If he weighed five pounds, she would be surprised. It was hard to imagine, but her babies would probably not be much bigger than this when they were born. They could be smaller, if they came earlier. "Is he pretty low maintenance at this stage?"

"In a way. He sleeps a lot, but because he's so small, we have to be sure to feed him every couple of hours. He gets tired fast so he doesn't take much at one time." Jordan paused, apparently thinking. "The last preemie we had was on an apnea monitor. That thing was a pain."

"That sounds a little…daunting." Especially since Lacey would have two at the same time. Even more daunting if she was doing it alone. But if she stayed with Devin, she would be staying because it was the right thing for all of them, not because she was desperate for help with twins. "Are you planning to keep fostering?"

"We're staying licensed for now, but we're taking a break until Essie turns a year old… at least. We stay busy enough just doing respite for Claire and Joe." She sighed. "I'm not a very good hostess these days. Sorry not to have lunch waiting when you got here. I do have some chicken salad and fruit in the refrigerator."

"Oh, it's fine. Trust me. I'm just glad to get out of the house for a little while. I haven't had a lot of time to make friends here, so it's nice to get to visit."

"How are things over at Triple Creek? It looked like the farm stand was going really well."

"I think it's going okay. I'm making zucchini brownies and those cookies you liked almost every day."

Jordan said, "They're so good. Hang on. Let me put Essie in her bed before we both die of hunger."

Her new friend disappeared into a door leading from the kitchen and returned just a couple of minutes later. Tugging open the refrigerator door, she looked back at Lacey. "I bet your kids are up on horseback before they're walking. You and Devin seem like such a good match."

To Lacey's horror, her eyes filled. Jordan stopped in the middle of the kitchen with an armful of food from the refrigerator. "Oh, no, I said the wrong thing. Hang on."

Jordan walked over to the farm table in the middle of their big open living area. She laid out chicken salad, a package of fresh fruit chunks and some crackers, returning to the kitchen for forks and paper plates. "I'm so not a hostess. I'm looking at this thinking it would all look better on some china."

Lacey sniffed and smiled, relieved that—for the moment, at least—Jordan had changed the subject. "I know you're kidding. I've been on the rodeo circuit for so many years. I wouldn't know what to do if someone put china in front of me."

With a laugh, Jordan pulled a couple of bottles of water from the refrigerator. "You knew just the right thing to say."

Putting a spoonful of chicken salad on her plate, Lacey said, "How did you and Ash get together?"

"You mean because we seem so mismatched? Trust me, no one was more surprised than I was. Levi was adopted from foster care and when he first came to me, he had some special medical needs. Ash was right there with me the whole time."

"That sounds amazing." Lacey took a bite of her chicken salad but her appetite disappeared as she thought about what a polar opposite her experience with Devin had been from Jordan's with Ash.

Jordan lifted a chunk of cantaloupe. "So, I'm just going to warn you that I'm nosy and opinionated, so stop me if I overstep. But I get the feeling that maybe you're not feeling so great right now?"

With a big sigh, Lacey considered her options. She needed a friend desperately, someone who could be objective about all the things. "Can I share with you in confidence?"

Jordan lifted a hand. "Wait here. I'll be right back." She went into the kitchen, pulled a container of chocolate ice cream from the freezer and grabbed two spoons from the drawer. "Here's the deal. My sisters and I have this rule. What is said when the ice cream is on the table is secret. Period."

How did Lacey share something so personal when she barely understood it herself? "So, Devin and I have been friends forever and that was all it was for a long time…until we had kind of a whirlwind romantic night. Devin proposed and we were in Vegas so we got married. Which I thought was great, until I woke up the next morning alone. And pregnant, as I found out a few weeks later."

Jordan pushed away her plate of chicken salad and pulled the ice cream container into the center of the table. "I think we're going to need this. I heard Devin went to rehab."

"He did and he's been sober for months now. I came to ask him for a divorce and found out that he didn't even remember the wedding. Since he found out about the babies coming, he's been great. I honestly can't tell you why I'm so terrified. But I am. Terrified."

Jordan took a spoonful of the ice cream. "I was reading about trauma recently—it's a big part of fostering—and I learned that the brain remembers things even when we don't have a conscious memory of them. Like, this thing happened and this is how I felt so I'm going to do everything I can to avoid that feeling again ever. The kids don't know why they're acting the way they are. It's mostly unconscious."

With her own spoon halfway to her mouth, Lacey narrowed her eyes. "So you're saying even if I think I want to trust Devin, my brain is telling me I should run because I was hurt before?"

"That's exactly it. When I was dating Ash, I was literally petrified that things were going to end badly and I was going to get my heart broken. And I was a new mom to Levi and I was afraid Levi would get *his* heart broken. I was a mess. I was so scared that I broke up with him."

"What?"

"I'm serious." The baby in the living room

started to whimper. Jordan dug through a diaper bag hanging on the chair next to her and pulled out a tiny bottle, breaking the seal and screwing a nipple onto the top. "Do you want to feed him?"

"If it's okay." Lacey watched Jordan, bottle in hand, as she picked Amos up from the bouncy seat. She seemed so confident in her skills, so at ease, even with this super tiny baby.

"Hey, little buddy, are you hungry? I bet you are." The baby was squirming, his face getting red when Jordan handed him to Lacey. She stuck the bottle in his mouth and he was soon eating happily.

Holding the baby gave her something to do, something to think about besides how insecure she felt right now. "So what changed that made you able to take a chance with Ash?"

Jordan drew her shoulders up with her breath and dug the spoon into the carton of ice cream one more time. "You're not going to like this—but, there's a tipping point, when the pain of being away from someone hurts worse than the heartbreak would if it even happened. I mean, if it's going to hurt anyway, you might as well be happy in the meantime, right?"

Lacey stared into her new friend's face. "I never thought about it that way. You're right."

The baby's bottle hissed as he sucked the last bit of milk out of it. Lacey looked up in panic.

Jordan said, "Just sit him up on your lap. Hold his head up with his chin between your thumb and pointy finger—there you go. Now pat his back. He's so new, he's still really limp."

Lacey patted Amos's back until he let out a little burp.

"See, you're a natural. So, are you in love with him?"

The question jerked her back to the conversation. She sighed. "I don't want to be in love with him."

Jordan smiled. "Yeah, that's not what I asked. I said I was nosy and opinionated, so here comes the opinion. If you love him, you have to tell him."

Her eyes on the baby's precious little face, Lacey said, "I don't know if I can do that."

With a shrug, Jordan said, "If it's gonna hurt anyway, what do you have to lose? Don't answer that. Just think about it."

"Thanks, Jordan. It helps to have your perspective." Honestly, it seemed like she had a lot to lose, but if she didn't try, she'd be depriving her babies of their dad without even giving him a real shot. She'd be depriving herself of her husband and Devin of his wife. "It's so hard to sort out."

"Your feelings are justified." When Lacey looked up, Jordan said, "They are. Without question. But if you want a future with him, you're going to have to forgive him. I'll be praying for you, my sweet friend. I know this isn't easy."

Those words lingered in Lacey's mind long after she handed the baby back to Jordan, gave her a hug and thanked her for the time together. She pulled into the driveway at Triple Creek Ranch and put the car in Park.

She'd been praying for wisdom and clarity. She'd prayed for relief from the fear that had plagued her ever since she found out she was pregnant.

He left her in Vegas, yes. And yes, she felt abandoned. But Devin wasn't her mom. It was a completely different situation with a completely different outcome. It was time for her to stop punishing Devin for what her mom had done.

So now, she prayed for the courage to trust him. If it was going to hurt anyway, what did she have to lose?

Chapter Sixteen

With his arm around Lacey's waist, Devin held his breath as they walked toward the hospital door. Lacey was whispering something under her breath and he didn't dare interrupt her as they inched forward. The last four weeks had been peaceful, idyllic almost, the routine of the long farm days calming in a strange way. Lacey had seemed content to simply be together, often joining him as he'd done his chores, pestering him to share stories about his childhood. He obliged her with the adventures of Tanner, Garrett and Devin. And they'd both managed to ignore the fact that the date of their babies' birth and their self-imposed deadline for a decision was coming soon.

He hadn't even wanted to mention the parenting class, but with a determined set to her chin, Lacey reminded him it was their last chance. She'd never backed away from a challenge as long as he'd known her and his admiration only grew as he watched her battle her fear and win. When they reached the door, she didn't look up. He opened the door and she walked through it.

A wall of cold air hit them in the face when they entered the building and her steps faltered, but he just kept going and her lips started moving again. A few seconds later, he opened the door to the classroom and they were inside. When he eased her into a chair close to the door, she looked up and took a deep breath.

He was so proud of her for not giving up. They weren't home free yet—they had the hospital tour to get through after class but, for the first time, he felt hopeful that they'd be able to do it. "You okay?"

Her face was still a little white, her hand a little clammy in his, but she nodded. "Now it's just any other classroom."

The teacher walked to the front of the room with a big toothy smile on her face. "Welcome to Magnificent Multiples! If you'll look in your complimentary diaper bag, you'll find that we've put together a notebook for you with lots of ideas for how to manage your multiples, whether you have two or three or more!"

Devin turned to Lacey with wide eyes and mouthed, "More?"

She shook her head and murmured, "I think I'm good with two, thanks."

The teacher walked them through the notebook, filling his head with all kinds of advice he didn't know he needed. Feeding schedule. Sleep schedule. Gender-neutral clothing because who wants to be figuring out if a onesie is pink or blue in the middle of the night? Not a lot of snaps because they take too long. And the best news of all… They could expect for their twins to go through six *thousand* diapers in the first year.

When Lacey squeezed his hand and said, "Breathe," he realized he'd been muttering out loud.

He didn't hear a lot after that. For his own sanity, it was probably better that he think about other things. He was planning to be involved in the care of the babies and he knew it was probably going to be hard, but some things? It was probably better to just not know.

"So, we're going to take a small break before we walk through the labor and delivery wing in the hospital." The teacher's bright, cheerful voice cut into his thoughts. He scowled. She could afford to be cheerful. She wasn't going to be buying six thousand diapers this year. "In your bag, you'll find some peanut butter crackers and a couple of small bottles of water. For a busy parent of multiples, it's just as important to keep your own energy up when you're out and about with your babies."

As Lacey handed him a package of crackers, she grinned. "Don't forget to pack your snacks, cowboy."

"I'll just add that to the long list of things I need to remember. My brain is tired." He pulled the plastic wrap apart and took out a cracker. "She didn't answer any of my questions."

"Like what?" Lacey looked amused, but he knew for a fact she'd been chasing that barrel-racing championship buckle when other girls were babysitting. She had little to no baby experience, just like him.

"Like what do you do if you're by yourself and both of them are crying at the same time? What if one of them's hungry and one of them's wet? Or one needs to burp and the other needs a nap? She didn't cover any of that stuff."

Her expression went from amused to concerned, her bottle of water halfway to her mouth. "You're right, she didn't. Those are very good questions."

He shrugged as he crunched on a cracker. "I guess we'll figure it out. In the meantime, we got some coupons and a diaper bag full of samples."

She put the bottle of water down and said firmly, "It's going to be fine."

He shot her a look. "Are you saying that to yourself or to me?"

"Both." She laughed as their facilitator cleared her throat in the doorway to the classroom.

"Okay, everyone, we're going on a little tour. We'll be visiting an empty L&D suite but there are people in the other ones, so remember to be respectfully quiet."

Lacey's expression turned wary. She sucked in a breath, and Devin remembered they weren't out of the woods yet.

He took her hand in his and helped her to her feet. "Don't overthink it. We're just going for a walk."

Lacey nodded, but her throat worked as she swallowed.

Waiting until the other expectant parents left the room to move into line behind them, he said, "Have you thought any more about names?"

She followed him into the hall, her eyes straight ahead, her hand wrapped around his in a painful grip. "You mean other than Elmo and Prudence?"

He smiled. "Yeah. But to be honest, I do kind of like those now that we've been calling them that."

"Not a chance are we naming our kids Elmo and Prudence. We could keep the initials, though, if we can think of something to go with them."

"Like Penelope or Patience?" He raised an eyebrow.

"Or Paul or Patrick for boys."

"Okay." He hung back as their leader scanned her badge across the reader mounted beside the double doors and the group entered the OB wing. "I see where you're going with this." He thought for a minute. "I like the name Phoebe. It's old-fashioned but feminine. It would sound good over the loudspeaker at the rodeo. Riding next is… Phoebe… Cole."

Lacey let out a shaky laugh as he dragged the syllables out like the announcer would. "You're right. It's cute. I say yes to Phoebe. Can we use Rose as a middle name? It's my grandmother's name and she helped raise me after my mom left."

"Phoebe Rose." He tried it out to see how it sounded together. "It sounds classy. It has meaning. I like it."

They stopped outside a glass window where a nurse in pink scrubs was wrapping a baby in a white blanket with pink and blue stripes. When she saw them in the window, she smiled and held up the baby, who looked like a burrito with fat baby cheeks.

"Oh, how precious." Lacey put her hand on the glass. "It's so hard to believe that we'll be seeing our babies very soon. In some ways, I'm so not ready. In others, that day can't get here fast enough."

"I feel the same way." He realized they were the only ones still loitering by the nursery window and reached for her arm. When she startled at his touch, he realized that while she was handling this better than he'd expected, she was still strung tight with anxiety. "You're doing great. We're going to make happy memories here."

Her eyes met his and she nodded. "You're right. I can do this. Let's go."

As they followed the group toward the other end of the hall, Devin said, "Do you have any thoughts about an E name for a boy? The only one I can think of is Elvis, but I think maybe that's a no?"

"Definite no on Elvis." As they waited to enter the maternity suite, her fingers tightened on his and she visibly focused on breathing.

"Let's go see where our babies are going to be born." As the group filed out, he stepped into the maternity suite with Lacey. He wasn't sure what he expected, but it was nice, set up kind of like a living room with warm wood tones and a sofa and chairs. The medical equipment was there but as unobtrusive as possible.

Lacey's grip on his hand loosened slightly as she looked around the room. "It looks pretty nice in here. We could bring one of the quilts from home and it would be even better."

Home. The word wound through his consciousness and came to rest somewhere in the vicinity of his heart, the feeling even more pronounced because he felt it, too. The farmhouse hadn't been home since his family died, but now, with Lacey there, it was home again.

She made it feel like home.

Devin grinned. "I agree. A quilt would be perfect. And maybe we could bring in some wildflowers and one of the cows, a few piglets…"

She elbowed him. "You are so annoying."

With a grin, he slung his arm around her shoulders. "Yeah, I know."

As they walked out to the car, she said, "What about Eli? It has a good solid sound. James Eli Cole?"

"James Eli? It's perfect. My mom would be tickled that we'll have a Sweet Baby James." He chuckled as he unlocked the truck and pulled open the door for her, holding her arm as she awkwardly got in. "Eli and Phoebe. It sounds right."

When she was fully in the truck, she turned to look at him. "Did we just name our babies?"

"I think we did. We are *such* good parents."

She was laughing when he closed the door. He paused for just a second to acknowledge the enormity of what they'd just accomplished. He closed his eyes, winging a quick prayer of thanks to God because after two months of false starts, they'd finally attended a class at the hospital.

And they had rocked it.

Turning the key in the ignition and starting the air-conditioning blowing, he realized he hadn't asked her... "So what exactly were you saying to yourself as you walked into the building?"

A bemused smile crossed her face. "I spent last night reading stories about women who've done incredible things—hard things—and telling myself that if those women could do those amazing things, I could do this. So as I was walking in, I was saying their names to myself. *Mother Teresa. Malala. Elizabeth Blackwell. Eleanor Roosevelt.* Like that."

Devin leaned over the armrest and kissed her temple. "They can't hold a candle to you. Let's go home."

And he smiled. Finally things were starting to go right.

Lacey was still smiling when Devin pulled up to the farm. She hadn't realized how alone she'd felt in her fear, but his easy acceptance had lifted that weight and made it possible for her to face it.

Tonight, walking in the doors of the hospital had been uncomfortable, but she'd known she could do it. And when they'd walked through the hospital to the labor and delivery, she'd been nervous, but he'd kept her mind occupied talking about the babies' names.

She rubbed her belly with both hands. Phoebe and Eli. She loved them so much.

"Why's the house dark?" Devin's eyes were on the farmhouse as he held his hands out and helped her slide out of the truck to the ground.

"I don't know." At almost thirty weeks pregnant, she was feeling so unwieldy, more and more off balance as the twins grew heavier. Devin's hand at her elbow steadied her as they started toward the house. "Did Tanner mention he had something to do tonight?"

"He didn't say anything to me." Devin walked up the steps and stuck his key in the lock, but the doorknob turned easily, the door pushing open. "Tanner? You here?"

Devin flipped on the lights. Tanner sat in the recliner, a pile of unread mail on the table beside him, an open letter in his lap, his face carved into lines that hadn't been there when they'd left for the hospital. Sadie lay at his feet.

Lacey didn't know what was going on but it couldn't be good. Tanner was not one for dramatics. He was the quiet, capable, *reasonable* one. If he was sitting in the dark, it had to be bad.

Devin sat down in the chair beside him, leaning forward, his elbows on his knees.

"I'll go make some coffee." Lacey started for the door.

"Stay. This affects you, too." Tanner's voice was raspy and strained.

She slowly turned around. "What's going on, Tanner?"

Devin's brother lifted the piece of paper from his lap and let it flutter to the ground. "The bank is foreclosing on the farm. They've given us thirty days to come up with the full amount of the loan or they're taking it."

"What! Why? We've been making payments!" Devin grabbed the paper from the floor and stared at it. "They can't do this."

"Yeah, they can. They started sending notices about six months ago that they were calling in the loan because the payments had been erratic. I was hoping they'd give us some more time since we're turning a small profit now, but they're not. We've lost the farm. *I* lost the farm."

"No, Tanner, that's not true. The farm is all of our responsibility. We let you down."

Devin's brother stood, his face expressionless. "You didn't let me down. Tomorrow I'll go to the bank and try to talk to them one more time, but I'm afraid we're out of chances unless we can somehow come up with ninety-seven thousand dollars."

"I have some money put aside and I can ask my dad if he could loan us the rest until the farm is profitable," Lacey offered hesitantly.

"No." Tanner and Devin said it at the same time, turning identical brown eyes to her.

"I figured that's what you would say, but if you change your mind, say the word and I'll make the call." At Devin's side, Lacey slid her hand into his.

He cleared his throat. "I think we need to pray. I know we're not really into talking about our faith—and that's okay, I'm not knocking it. But this… It seems important to me."

Tanner shook his head. "I'm not sure prayers are gonna do a lot of good now, Dev."

"Humor me." Devin held out a hand to his brother, who reluctantly took it. Lacey held hers out, and Tanner gripped it with his work-worn hand. She couldn't imagine how he felt. He'd worked so hard.

Devin bowed his head and took a deep breath. "Dear God, I'm not good at this kind of stuff. But this is about family. It's about home. It's about a foundation for our future. We need You, God, and we pray if it's Your will that You would help us find a way to save the farm. Help us to trust You no matter what the answer is. Amen."

There was a sheen in Tanner's eyes when they looked up. He cleared his throat. "Thanks, Devin. I'm going up to bed now."

His footsteps heavy, Tanner climbed the stairs, leaving Devin and Lacey still holding hands in the middle of the living room.

"Hey." Lacey wrapped her arms around Devin's waist, holding on as he pulled her closer, looking into his steady brown eyes. "I just want you to know I love you. I've always loved you. I know I haven't been fair to you, but I'm trying."

She wasn't sure when things had shifted—it had happened so gradually—but she knew that he could do it. He wasn't just acting like a victim of something that had happened to him. He'd consistently chosen the path that had brought him closer to the man that she had always known he could be.

He reached up and brushed her hair away

from her face with a gentle hand. "You can have as long as you need. I'm not going anywhere. I want to be a husband and a dad. I love you."

Up to this point, their lives had been spent waiting for that eight seconds or fourteen seconds in the arena, and their lives weren't better when they did that. They were always looking for that next record-breaking ride, the next high point. And yeah, they'd accomplished some amazing things, but they'd missed so many moments, looking into the future, just waiting.

She didn't want to miss the moments anymore.

They were too precious.

"Your prayer was perfect. It was the right thing to do." She didn't want to move from his arms. His hand rested on her belly where their babies were growing and she suddenly wanted her children to grow up in this house. To run in the fields and swing on a rope swing into the spring-fed pond.

He sighed again, his arms tightening around her. "It's all I know to do. We've worked as hard as we can work. We're out of options. Now we have to believe that if God wants us to be here, He'll provide a way."

Chapter Seventeen

The sky was deep purple, with just a hint of orange in the west, when Devin headed to the barn with a bottle for Nemo. He found Garrett already in the barn feeding ravenous baby goats.

Garrett looked up without a smile, eliciting an angry butt from one of the babies when the nipple slipped out of its mouth. "How're you doing?"

"Not good. You?"

"Not good. Not since I talked to Tanner this morning. I put my house in town on the market a few hours ago but I doubt it'll sell in time to make a difference. It's worth a shot, I guess, but even then, it's not going to bring in the kind of money we need to stave off the bank."

"I don't have anything left to sell." Devin paused, earning a firm nudge from Nemo for his inattention. "Unless maybe I could sell Reggie."

"No. We don't sell family members."

"Without a farm, he won't have a place to live anyway." Devin paused, grief at the thought of losing their home settling like a weight on his shoulders. He'd imagined raising his kids here. Growing old with his brothers. It wasn't just a house. Their future was on the line. "We could sell off the cattle, but it would take years to recover from the loss of the herd, which wouldn't solve anything."

"We don't need ways to make income now. We need an influx of capital. I knew money was tight, but this is bad. I can't believe we didn't know." Garrett held the bottles up higher so the baby goats could get to the last little bit. "Okay, okay, here you go, you little beggars."

"I guess Tanner wanted to fix it so we didn't have to worry about it. He's always been that way. He tried to get me to come home after I hurt my ankle so he could take care of me. He was right, but I wasn't having it."

Garrett sighed. "Well, you have to be

ready to make a big change like that. And now you're married to Lacey and about to have twins, so what would you do different anyway?"

Devin turned incredulous eyes on Garrett. "Dude. So many things I would do different."

"Fair point." The kids sucked the bottles dry and Garrett pulled them away, eliciting bleats from the little goats.

Nemo was a slow drinker compared with the goats. One of them tried to jump up and steal the calf's bottle. Devin nudged it away with one leg, amused at its tenacity when it immediately tried again.

Devin was pretty sure he already knew what Garrett would say about his proposal, but he was going to talk to him about it anyway because they were all in this together.

Still, he hesitated. He'd come so far in repairing the relationship with his brothers and the last thing he wanted to do was damage it again. "So…"

Garrett looked up.

"I got an email last night around midnight. There's an invitational rodeo in Colorado Springs this weekend. The purse is a hundred thousand dollars." He kept his eyes on the hungry calf, not quite able to make eye contact with Garrett.

His brother sat back on his heels. "That sounds like a terrible idea if you're thinking about it. You're well past the deadline to enter anyway."

Nemo finished his bottle and Devin pulled the towel scrap from where it rested over his shoulder and wiped the foamy milk residue from the little calf's face. "That's the thing. It's been booked for weeks, but one of the riders broke his shoulder blade in training yesterday and they want a full roster. They emailed me to see if I was interested."

"It's not worth it."

"What's not worth it?" Tanner's voice broke into their conversation. He stood in the doorway to the stall, the keys to the ATV in one hand, a travel mug of coffee in the other.

Devin shot Garrett a look. He wasn't ready to talk about this with Tanner. Not yet.

Garrett shook his head. "Devin's thinking about riding in the invitational this weekend."

"That's about the dumbest thing I've ever heard." Tanner walked closer. "You could lose your foot. You have a wife and two babies to think about. I suggest you put them first."

"How do I put them first if we lose the

farm and I can't support them?" He'd been trying to shove it down all day but the panic rose like bile in Devin's throat.

He did have a wife and two babies counting on him. How could he turn down a chance to save their livelihood? The livelihood of his older brother and the family home for all of them?

"I've got to get out of here." Devin gave Nemo a final scratch behind the ears, grabbed his cane and started for the house, Garrett right in step with him. Devin cocked a glance at his brother. "Where do you think you're going?"

"I'm going in the kitchen with you because I'm hungry and because I want to make sure you tell your wife about this craziness."

"I'll tell her, but I'll tell her when I'm ready. Now get out of my way. I'm going to cook some supper."

When he entered the living room, Lacey was just coming out of the kitchen. She had her hair in one of those loose bun things. Tendrils fell around her face, which was pink from the warmth of the stove. His heart filled to overflowing with love for her. It stopped him in his tracks—the inexplicable, overwhelming feelings he had for this woman.

"I just stuck some corn bread in the oven and I got the greens Tanner picked simmering. I have cookies to make tonight, so I thought I'd put my feet up for a few minutes while the corn bread is in the oven. What are you guys up to? Feeding time?"

Garrett gave Devin a pointed look. "What's going on, Devin?"

"Devin?" Lacey turned toward him, concern in her eyes. "Are you okay?"

"I'm fine. I got an email asking me to compete in the invitational in Colorado Springs this weekend. They had a late withdrawal and they want to fill the roster."

"You're not going to do it, though, right?" She'd gone very still, one arm curving around her belly in a protective gesture.

"I..."

Garrett interjected. "Why are you even considering this? The only sane answer is 'No, I'm not going to do it.'"

"Devin?" Lacey's eyes were steady on his. "Why would you risk it? You've come so far."

Garrett turned his gaze to Devin, as well. "Why would you risk it, Devin?"

Devin closed his eyes and sucked in a breath, counting to ten so he wouldn't yell at his brother. He gave up before he reached six. "Garrett, get out. Go fix yourself a sand-wich at your own house and let me talk to my wife."

"There's no food at my house." With a scowl, Garrett turned and stalked toward the front door.

"You should've thought of that before you tried to pick a fight between me and Lacey."

The door closed behind Garrett, who was still muttering. "Try to do the right thing by your brother and what do you get? Nothing. Not even a crumb of corn bread."

"Sometimes I wonder how I have the same DNA as those two. We couldn't be more different." He walked into the kitchen. "Do you want to have some tea and talk?"

She nodded and he pulled two glasses out of the cabinet and poured sweet tea over ice. He set her glass in front of the chair she'd settled into at the kitchen table and got the lemon out of the refrigerator for her.

Hashing out the offer with Lacey about competing in the invitational was not high on his list of things he wanted to do. In fact, he couldn't think of many things he wanted to do less, but he was learning. Hiding from issues and problems didn't mean they didn't exist. It just meant putting off the pain until later. And sometimes waiting meant the pain was going to be a whole lot worse than it would've been if he'd just dealt with it in the first place.

"So tell me about the offer." She looked down to where her hands cupped the cold glass, her lashes hiding her eyes.

"Any other time, I wouldn't consider it. I know you've had your doubts, but I've made my peace with retiring. I'll leave that to you and our kids, if they want to rodeo, but… This invitational has a grand prize of one hundred thousand dollars."

She nodded slowly. "That money would save the farm."

"It would."

"If you won."

"Yeah." That outcome was far from a given. He hadn't been on a bucking horse in months. He was the current titleholder and he could assume with some degree of certainty that he had the muscle memory to pull it off, but even in top shape, sometimes the best riders still got thrown. "There's no guarantee."

"I don't want you to do it. I'm scared. And it's not just me being scared for you. I'm scared for what it means for our kids."

He nodded, hoping Lacey didn't notice his fingers clenching around his glass. "I know."

"I understand if you feel you have to, but I'm begging you not to do it, Devin. Please don't take that chance. There has to be another way to save the farm."

"If there is I haven't thought of it yet."

"You will." Lacey's eyes were so dark, he could barely see her pupils, but he could see the storm of turmoil in them. He reached for her hand and pulled her to her feet and into his arms, feeling the tension in her as she battled for control.

"Can I say one thing?"

She nodded and he took her hand, placing it over his heart. "I know it's tempting to be reminded of how you've been hurt before. Maybe when you feel that doubt creeping in, just remember you're the one this heart beats for. I'll always come back, Lacey, I promise. Can you just promise you'll trust me? Please?"

She hesitated but lifted one shoulder and let it drop. "I can promise I'll try."

"Let's eat supper and then you've got to get some rest and so do I. No one got any sleep last night. But no matter what happens, we're going to have a lot of work to do around here."

He tipped her face toward his and pressed a kiss to her lips, almost losing it when he felt them tremble under his. "I love you."

"I love you, too."

Trust me.

He prayed that he would be trustworthy, that she would see him that way. The words were easy to say and so hard to live up to. But somehow he had to find a solution to what they were facing as a family.

Somehow he had to find a way.

Lacey lumbered out of bed at four forty-five the next morning. Sleep was getting more and more impossible the bigger the babies got. In the adjoining bathroom, she splashed cold water on her face and looped her long brown hair into a loose bun on her head. She was almost positive she'd heard Devin in the kitchen making breakfast. He wasn't sleeping either, apparently.

And no wonder. It was hard to imagine a worse scenario for a ranch family than losing the ranch. They'd had some hard times on their ranch growing up, but she didn't think they'd ever come close to losing it.

She didn't blame them for being tied up in knots about it. Suddenly not knowing where she'd be taking her babies home from the hospital was a little disconcerting, to say the least.

Following the scent of coffee into the kitchen, she went straight to the pot. She poured herself a cup and grabbed a biscuit from the stove, taking a bite as she turned toward the table. Her motions slowed as she saw a familiar stack of papers.

It was the divorce papers she'd brought with her, the ones that Devin had said he wouldn't sign unless she stayed until the babies were born.

Her first reaction was a flash of anger. She'd been abandoned before... Why should she expect him to be any different? He'd wanted to prove to her that he could change. That he could be a better person.

She picked up the papers and turned to the back page, even though she had a feeling she knew what she was going to find.

And she did find it. His dark scrawl on the very last page.

She sank down into the kitchen chair and stared at the signatures on the page that meant they were divorced. She felt the acid rise in her throat as fear bloomed in her heart.

She saw just the corner of a small yellow

sticky note between the pages and pulled it out. In the same dark scrawl it said, *Please trust me, Lacey.*

Had he just been pretending to be content with being a family man? Or had she been the one pretending…pretending to give him another chance?

Holding the note in her hand, she realized the anger and fear had drained away, leaving her numb. She had no idea how she felt. She needed air.

Picking up her coffee, she started out to the front porch as Tanner came down the stairs. "Is he gone?"

"Yes."

"I thought I heard the truck start up. I'm so sorry, Lacey. I don't know what to say."

"He signed the divorce papers." She had to swallow hard, but the words still barely rasped out. "And he left a note that said to trust him."

Tanner didn't say anything, just shook his head and went into the kitchen. A few seconds later, she heard the chink of a ceramic mug hitting the countertop and coffee splashing in it.

She continued to the porch with her own mug of coffee, walking out into the pre-sun-rise quiet. A rooster crowed from the back-yard and she wondered if he was confused by the humans being awake already.

Her feelings were so confused, her heart literally aching in her chest. She didn't know what to believe. Devin had shown her again and again over the course of the last few months that he'd changed. That he *was* a person she could trust. Still, she couldn't help but feel abandoned once again. Hurt and confused again. And once again, he'd gone without a word, leaving a document behind.

Just over seven months ago it had been their marriage certificate. This morning it was their divorce papers. And what did that even mean? Had he signed them because he was breaking their agreement and planning to do something he knew she wouldn't approve of?

Please trust me, he'd said. How did she trust him when he had all the power? But did he? From the beginning, she'd been the one who wanted to end things. He'd been the one holding on to a marriage that seven months ago hadn't even existed except on paper.

Maybe by signing the divorce papers, he was giving her the power to rewrite the script. Giving her the power to be the one who walked away. Giving her the choice.

She closed her eyes, her mind drifting back to the moment in the kitchen when he'd placed her hand on his chest. That strong, steady heartbeat under her hand.

Walking to the porch swing, she sat down, letting her feet lift off the floor as it swung back with her weight. Out of the corner of her eye, she saw something on the far end of the swing and she reached for it. It was Devin's Bible. She'd seen him reading it just yesterday.

She ran her hand over the smooth surface, the pages curling in the summer humidity. It was getting ragged, the color of the leather worn from use. She opened it and realized that the inside pages were filled with notes and tabs and bookmarks in Devin's handwriting.

She turned to the first one. Psalm 139. *I praise you for I am fearfully and wonderfully made.*

Her throat began to ache as she turned to the next tab. 2 Corinthians. *For when I am weak, then I am strong.*

Tears gathered in her eyes as she turned to the next marker in Titus 3. *He saved us not because of works done by us in righteousness but according to his own mercy... So that being justified by his grace we might become heirs...*

Faster now, she turned to Ephesians 2, tears streaming down her face. *For we are his workmanship.*

Galatians 3:26. *You are all children of God through faith...* And in Devin's hand in the margin, she saw that he'd written *It's not who I think I am, it's who God says I am. God says I am His.*

God says I am His.

Slowly, she closed the book. As she lifted her coffee and took a trembling sip, she watched pink dawn spread slowly up the darkness, the stars winking out one by one as light filled the sky. How did she trust that the sun would come up each morning? Because it had for all the days of her life?

How did she trust a God she couldn't see? Because even in her darkest moments, she knew that there was hope. Day after day, she was reminded of His goodness and faithfulness. Even when she didn't understand her circumstances.

The front door opened and Tanner stepped outside. He walked to the porch rail and leaned on it, his mug of coffee in his hand. "I tried to call him. He didn't pick up. What do you want to do?"

She wasn't confused anymore. She wasn't numb. She knew. "What I really want to do… is believe him when he says trust me."

He shot her a look. "Past experience says that's a horrible idea."

She sighed and wiped her face of the tears that had fallen as she'd read the verses in Devin's Bible. "I know."

Tanner sighed, his eyes still on hers. "Are you going to call him?"

"No." She hesitated. "For some reason he needs time and I…need to give it to him. If we're really going to make our relationship work, I have to be able to trust him. I do trust him."

It was a terrifying feeling, like wading into the deep water and not knowing if the undertow would sweep you away or if the waves would gently nudge you back to shore where the warm sand and the safety waited.

But Devin had fought hard. She knew he hadn't made this decision lightly. She wanted to trust him. And she believed in him. So she did.

Chapter Eighteen

Five days after Devin left in the middle of the night, Lacey heard the television come on in the living room and her heart rate immediately skyrocketed. The invitational rodeo was tonight.

Tanner had repeatedly tried to reach Devin with no response other than a short text that said, I'm fine. Trust me.

He'd checked in with her by text twice a day, morning and evening, to make sure she was doing okay. She wanted to ask where he was and what he was doing, but she didn't. He'd asked for her trust.

She was trying to give it to him. But the longer she waited, the more worried she got. She prayed that he was attending meetings, that he was getting enough sleep. He'd been under so much stress. Was he sticking with the lifestyle changes that had helped him on the path to wellness or was he back in that old environment and tempted to give in to the lure of old habits?

He'd signed the divorce papers. And she couldn't help but ask herself what he was planning for her, for their unborn babies. But every time she wondered if he'd somehow changed his mind about wanting to build a family together, she remembered him placing her hand on his heart and promising he would always come back.

Tanner had placed a plate of cold cuts, fruit and vegetables on the coffee table in front of the couch, but the idea of eating right now made her feel sick.

Even so, when the rodeo started with the national anthem, she felt a wave of nostalgia. She'd been competing since she was a preteen and the rodeo, in many ways, was home to her.

On television, the announcer said, "We were sad to hear that Travis Montrose won't be competing tonight due to a broken shoulder blade during practice earlier this week. The latest report from his family is that he's recuperating well after surgery and promises to be here next year."

There was no mention of Devin filling in.

A band of muscles tightened across her stomach, a quick rush of pain catching her off guard and stealing her breath. She closed her eyes, waiting it out. Obviously, sitting here was doing her no good. She pushed to her feet. "I need to get some air. Call me if you see Devin."

Grabbing a handful of carrots from the kitchen, she walked outside into the balmy Southern night. The cicadas were singing and a soft breeze was blowing. She focused on the sound of the animals in the field. It felt so peaceful compared with the turmoil brewing inside her.

She walked to the edge of the pasture, and Dolly took a few timid steps toward her. A carrot held out in Lacey's flat hand was the deciding factor and the sweet mare stuck her head over the fence for a treat. "Hey, girl. Are you feeling a little lonely?"

Dolly looked at her with big velvet brown eyes.

"Yeah, me, too." Walking toward the barn, Lacey pressed a hand into her back where it ached. She was carrying so much weight in the front that her back had been killing her all day. She focused on breathing, on the random flicker of the fireflies across the pasture. One. Two...

Despite Devin's absence, despite everything, she could take in the beauty of a quiet country night. She could appreciate that she belonged here. He belonged here, too. She whispered the words. "Protect him, please, God. Bring him home safely."

As if He had heard her pleas, the rattle of a horse trailer and the growly engine of a truck reached her ears as it turned into the drive. She barely dared to hope that it was Devin, even as an expectant feeling rose in her chest. Her hands went to her stomach where their twins were kicking. *Please, God, let it be Devin.*

His old truck pulled to a stop near the barn. She let out the breath she'd been holding—it was him.

Lacey rushed toward the truck, meeting him as he slid out of the cab and onto the ground. He took a step and caught her up in his arms, burying his face in her hair. "You stayed."

"Of course I stayed."

"You didn't call me." He put his arm around

her as they walked toward the porch. "I was afraid you were mad."

"I knew you needed space to do what you needed to do."

"What did I do to deserve you?" He stopped walking when they reached the glow of the porch light and turned to look at her. She studied his face. He looked tired, his beard a little stubbly, his eyes weary but clear, and she was so happy to see him.

She laughed, the sound winging into the wind and with it her worries about Devin. She still had no idea where they would be living in a month, but he was safe at home. "Clearly, you don't deserve me. I've been a wreck since you left."

"I'm sorry, Lacey. I felt like I had to do something to help save the farm. And I wanted you to have the space to walk away, if you wanted to. I hoped you wouldn't."

He turned to face her, holding her two hands in his. "I want to get the words right but I don't know if I can. I'm so—um—emotional. I've been practicing."

With another laugh, she leaned forward and kissed him. He dropped one of her hands and cupped her face, his whole body relaxing into hers, bringing her into the curve of his embrace. He sighed.

"That is not helping me clear my thoughts." He took a step back, pressing his hands together as if he were praying, and took a deep bolstering breath.

He released it, holding his hands out, palms open to her as if he couldn't do anything else. "You have my heart, Lacey. From the moment I saw you standing in the driveway with those awful divorce papers, I knew that you and I could have the greatest adventure together. I don't need the spotlight. I don't need the risk and the thrill. I need you. Just you."

Lacey's eyes filled, her vision blurring.

"I had a lot of time to think on the drive. I realized I was afraid of losing hold of who I was, but it's past time to let go of all that old shame I felt, all the things I tried to push down and hide. And I have to put away old dreams that don't fit me anymore."

She placed her hands in his and he held them tightly, looking down at her with the most tender expression. "I trust that we're going to build new dreams. Together."

As they stood in the warm circle of light from the porch, he let go of her hand and dug in his pocket. She gasped as he pulled out a ring. She recognized her grandma Rose's diamond ring immediately. "Devin, how...?"

"Your dad gave it to me. I went to ask his permission to ask you for your hand in marriage. I want to do it right this time." He looked down with a smile and tossed her words from months ago back to her. "In the right order."

Kneeling down, he held one of her hands and held the ring up with the other. "Lacey Elizabeth Jenkins, I love you and I promise to love you for the rest of my life. Through everything. Mountaintops and valleys, kids and dogs, rain and sunshine. I promise I will never give up on our love."

Containing her tears was not even a possibility as he said, "Will you do me the honor of becoming my wife? Officially?"

Lacey held out her hand and he slid the ring onto her finger. She looked down at the old ring and back to Devin's eyes, her gaze catching on his and holding it. "I was so afraid of being hurt again. But I realized after you left the other day that if I had to choose between safety and love, there was no contest. I choose love. A safe life without you is not a life I want. I trust you and I will always love you. Now, please, come here?"

"So that's a yes?" He stood with a laugh as she grabbed his head and pulled his lips to meet hers.

"Yes!" She dropped her head to his shoulder and stood in his embrace, letting happiness and hope for their future wash over her, his solid strength reminding her that together they could face anything. "Yes. Yes. Yes."

A throat cleared behind them. Devin lifted his head with a smile. His brother stood on the porch, a wary expression on his face.

Devin sighed. "Well, I guess you know I didn't win a hundred thousand dollars."

"I figured that when I didn't see you ride tonight." Tanner took the steps in his slow, steady way. "It's all right. We'll figure something out. I'll go let Reggie into the pasture."

Devin put a hand out to stop Tanner. "Actually that's not Reggie."

His brother turned slowly around, his eyes narrowing. "Where's Reggie?"

Devin took a few steps toward the trailer. "Being asked to participate in the invitational shook something loose in my brain that I should've thought about a long time ago. Sure, I'm a rodeo champ, but Reggie's a rodeo champ in his own right." He shrugged, with a half smile. "Lacey's dad helped me line up five ranchers who are willing to pay a steep price to have Reggie sire a foal. It's not a hundred thousand dollars, but maybe it's enough to negotiate more time with the bank."

Unemotional, practical Tanner had tears standing in his eyes. He cleared his throat again, a perplexed expression on his face as he tried to figure out what to do with all the stuff he must be feeling.

Devin hugged his brother, who'd been the one to give him another chance, and he was so grateful that he could be the one to give Tanner one. "I know you aren't sure you can count on me yet. It's okay. I'll be right here, pulling my weight. It's about time."

Tanner gave a short nod and looked away, his fist pressed to his lips. When he looked back, his voice was thick with emotion. "If that's not Reggie, who is it?"

Devin walked to the end of the trailer and opened it. He walked into the trailer, speaking softly to the patient horse inside. "Come on, beautiful girl. Someone's waiting to see you."

As he backed her out of the trailer, Lacey gasped. She dug one of the carrots from her pocket and held it out for her horse as Devin led her forward. "It's Magpie. Oh, sweet girl, I'm so glad to see you."

"Your dad and I thought Magpie might be a good pasture buddy for Dolly." His heart was so full—the expression on Lacey's face more than worth the trouble it had been to bring her horse to Alabama.

Lacey gasped, grabbing her belly, leaning forward with a low groan.

Devin was at her side in an instant, his arm around her, holding her steady. "Babe? What's going on?"

"It's okay." Her eyes still closed, she ground the words through her teeth. "This has been going on all day. I'm fine."

Tanner took Magpie's lead rope and guided her toward the barn as Lacey grabbed Devin's hand, her grip nearly cutting the circulation off.

She looked up with panic on her face. "It's too early. We're barely even thirty weeks yet. We can't have the babies. I won't do it."

Devin looked up and nodded at Tanner as he came out of the barn. "We need to go. Now."

His brother dug his keys out of his pocket and ran to his truck, turning it quickly and pulling up next to them.

Devin helped Lacey into the back seat of the truck and jumped in beside her as Tanner sped out of the driveway toward the hospital.

His heart was racing, thoughts throbbing in his head like an ache that wouldn't go away. He'd just figured it all out. They were just getting started. He loved Lacey and he loved their babies and there was absolutely nothing he could do at this point to help them. He wanted to cry, but there were no tears. Nothing except Lacey and their babies.

Devin slid his hands across her belly, shocked to feel how tight it was, and he knew he would give anything to switch places with her.

Please let them be okay, Lord. Let all of them be okay.

He murmured into her ear, "I'm gonna be right there with you every step of the way. I love you, Lacey. I'm not going to leave you. I promise. We're doing this together."

Lacey opened her eyes slowly, wincing as she pushed up in the bed. The last five weeks had gone so slowly as she'd remained in the hospital on bed rest, doing everything possible to keep the twins inside and growing. But last night they'd delivered two healthy babies who were breathing without oxygen and holding their own.

She looked to the left and chuckled as she saw Devin asleep in the very uncomfortable recliner he'd been in almost constantly since she'd arrived five weeks ago. But they'd made it. Thirty-five weeks and one day.

A whimper came from a bassinet by the window. Devin shot to his feet. "What? Which baby is it?"

"That's Eli. Phoebe's in the corner."

Devin walked to the bassinet and looked down. "Hey, buddy. Did you kick out of your swaddle? Let's see what we can do about that."

Like a pro—because he'd been practicing with the nurses for five weeks now—he snuggled Eli back into his burrito wrap and lifted him gingerly into his arms. "I can't get over how tiny he is. How much did he weigh again?"

"Five-one. Right? And Phoebe Rose was five-four?"

As if she'd heard her name, Phoebe started stirring in her bassinet. Devin passed the little baby bundle that was Eli to Lacey and crossed the room to Phoebe. He rewrapped her and picked her up, tucking a pacifier that covered nearly her whole face into her mouth. He walked to the bed, swaying gently and crooning to the baby.

Lacey laughed. "You are in so much trouble with that one."

"Why do you say that? I haven't been shopping for a pony yet...okay, I made a few calls, but that's all." He grinned at her. "I know I'm probably going to regret saying this because now that they're here, it isn't going to get easier. They're going to be yelling at us frequently and vehemently at least through their teenage years... But I'm just so glad to meet them."

She looked down into the tiny face of her baby boy, who she imagined would look exactly like Devin when he grew up. He had thick curly brown hair and dark lashes, and he already had her heart, just like his daddy did.

Meeting Devin's gaze, she said, "I love you."

Devin eased down to the side of the bed. "I love you, too. These last few months have been..." He stopped, cleared his throat. "These last few months have been more than I could ever deserve. I'm grateful for every minute, even the awful ones."

The door pushed open with a soft knock, and Tanner stuck his head in. "Y'all up for visitors?"

He had a plate wrapped in tinfoil, and Lacey's eyes snagged on it immediately. "What's that?"

"Just some zucchini brownies, if you're not sick of them. I used your recipe."

"They're good, too," Garrett interjected, as he came into the room, followed by Lacey's dad, Logan Jenkins.

"Hey, Dad, come meet your grandbabies."

Logan crossed to where his daughter reclined in the bed and rubbed her head. "Can't wait."

"Eli, this is Grandpop." She held Eli up for a kiss and her dad obliged, lifting him from her hands and kissing the tiny, fuzzy head.

The rancher's eyes were suspiciously damp. "Pleased to meet you, Eli."

Logan passed the baby to Garrett, who looked down in awe. "Wow, he's so little. He does kind of look like you, though, Devin. I think it's that scrunched-up expression. Or maybe the pointy head."

"You're so funny." Devin scowled. "I hope all you people used the hand sanitizer before you came in here."

Garrett raised an eyebrow at Logan. "I told you he was going to be giving orders."

"They're beautiful babies. Congratulations, guys." Tanner laid the plate of brownies on the counter and slid out the door.

Lacey looked up, meeting Devin's eyes. He shook his head slightly. "It's just gonna take time."

Her dad held his hands out for Phoebe Rose, and as he looked into her face, his eyes filled with tears again. "Your great-grandma Rose would be so proud to know you."

Drawing in a shaky breath, Lacey was almost relieved when the nurse came in to shoo out the visitors so they could do her vitals check. "We'll see you guys a little later."

After Garrett and Logan handed the babies back to their parents and left the room, the nurse turned back and winked at Lacey. "I'll be back in a few. Catch your breath."

Devin put a sleeping Phoebe in her bassinet, reached for Eli and tucked him back into place, before settling on the bed beside Lacey. "You holding up okay?"

"I'm tired but I feel good. I think it'll probably take some time to get my stamina up again."

"We're going to be tired for a long time."

He looked down at her with a twinkle in his eye. "Worth it."

"Every second." She lifted her hand into the air for a high five, the diamond ring he'd given her sparkling on her finger. "Up top?"

A fleeting smile crossed his face as tenderness filled his gaze and he leaned forward, giving her a gentle kiss on the lips. "Already there, Lace. I'm already there."

Epilogue

Two months later

Lacey held Devin's hand as they slowly rocked on the porch swing, the baby monitor beside them. It was a warm night for November, still in the sixties, and Lacey was barefoot, one foot sticking out from under the quilt he'd tossed over them when they'd sunk to the swing in exhaustion.

"Do you have any regrets?" Her voice was soft and sleepy.

He looked down at her in surprise. "In general? Sure."

She nudged him with her elbow. "That is not what I'm talking about."

"I definitely have some regrets about inviting a hundred people out here for a wedding this afternoon. I thought they were never going to leave when the dancing started."

Lacey laughed. "That's not what I mean, either."

"My only regret is not realizing sooner that the night we spent in Vegas was the first night of the best part of my life. I love you, Lace."

"Our life is different. No buzzers, no screaming crowds, no records being broken..."

There was an unspoken question in the words and he didn't even have to think about the answer. He lifted a finger. "Now, wait a minute—I'm pretty sure that Eli broke the record for diapers used in one day just yesterday."

"Our leaderboard consists of most ounces consumed and who has the fastest time getting a burp out of a baby." She laughed again and let her head fall back against his shoulder. "I don't miss it, always chasing that next hundredth of a second. I never knew I could be so happy."

He kissed her hair and just rocked, listening to the sounds of the farm slowly go to sleep. The cows were rustling in the field. One of the horses nickered softly. The confused rooster crowed in the backyard and Lacey stirred.

"I love you," his wife murmured sleepily. He pulled her closer into his embrace and thanked the Lord for his good fortune.

Because he was finally home.

* * * * *

If you loved this story,
check out the Family Blessings series,
from author Stephanie Dees

The Dad Next Door
A Baby for the Doctor
Their Secret Baby Bond
The Marriage Bargain

Available now from Love Inspired!
Find more great reads at
www.LoveInspired.com

Dear Reader,

Life is complicated. We make decisions with consequences. Things happen and we're left to deal with them the best we can. That's the case with Lacey and Devin. Their situation was their own doing—and they took responsibility—but their actions had their roots in the past, for both of them. The moment Lacey showed up in Red Hill Springs was a touchstone in their life, one of those rare instances when you know that what you choose to do in this moment could change your future forever.

I've had defining moments like that. Some of them I didn't know were turning points until later. Some I knew immediately would change my life. Some I've accepted with grace and some I have raged against. I try to remember every single day—because we have no idea when one of those life-changing moments will happen—that no matter what storms come I'm loved by God and His love is not conditional. *His* opinion is the one that matters. And no matter what I'm walking through, I know He's there, walking with me.

I know you've had to face unexpected challenges in your life. I've come to realize (with maturity, ha-ha) that everyone does. No one has a perfect life. But regardless of our circumstances, we can make the best of what we've got because we aren't going it alone.

You have my prayers, always, my friends, and I love hearing from you. You can contact me via mywebsite, www.stephaniedees. com, on Facebook at www.facebook.com/authorstephaniedees and in the reader group at www.facebook.com/groups/LIauthorsandreaders.

With love,
Stephanie

Get 4 FREE REWARDS!

We'll send you 2 FREE Books
<u>plus</u> 2 FREE Mystery Gifts.

Love Inspired® Suspense books feature Christian characters facing challenges to their faith... and lives.

FREE
Value Over
$20

Get 4 FREE REWARDS!

We'll send you 2 FREE Books plus 2 FREE Mystery Gifts.

Harlequin® Heartwarming™ Larger-Print books feature traditional values of home, family, community and—most of all—love.

FREE Value Over $20

THE FORTUNES OF TEXAS COLLECTION!

18 FREE BOOKS in all!

Treat yourself to the rich legacy of the Fortune and Mendoza clans in this remarkable 50-book collection. This collection is packed with cowboys, tycoons and Texas-sized romances!

YES! Please send me **The Fortunes of Texas Collection** in Larger Print. This collection begins with 3 FREE books and 2 FREE gifts in the first shipment. Along with my 3 free books, I'll also get the next 4 books from The Fortunes of Texas Collection, in LARGER PRINT, which I may either return and owe nothing, or keep for the low price of $5.24 U.S./$5.89 CDN each plus $2.99 for shipping and handling per shipment*. If I decide to continue, about once a month for 8 months I will get 6 or 7 more books but will only need to pay for 4. That means 2 or 3 books in every shipment will be FREE! If I decide to keep the entire collection, I'll have paid for only 32 books because 18 books are FREE! I understand that accepting the 3 free books and gifts places me under no obligation to buy anything. I can always return a shipment and cancel at any time. My free books and gifts are mine to keep no matter what I decide.

☐ 269 HCN 4622   ☐ 469 HCN 4622

Name (please print)

Address   Apt. #

City   State/Province   Zip/Postal Code

Mail to the **Reader Service:**
IN U.S.A.: P.O. Box 1341, Buffalo, N.Y. 14240-8531
IN CANADA: P.O. Box 603, Fort Erie, Ontario L2A 5X3

*Terms and prices subject to change without notice. Prices do not include sales taxes, which will be charged (if applicable) based on your state or country of residence. Canadian residents will be charged applicable taxes. Offer not valid in Quebec. All orders subject to approval. Credit or debit balances in a customer's account(s) may be offset by any other outstanding balance owed by or to the customer. Please allow three to four weeks for delivery. Offer available while quantities last. © 2018 Harlequin Enterprises Limited. ® and ™ are trademarks owned and used by the trademark owner and/or its licensee.

Your Privacy—The Reader Service is committed to protecting your privacy. Our Privacy Policy is available online at www.ReaderService.com or upon request from the Reader Service. We make a portion of our mailing list available to reputable third parties that offer products we believe may interest you. If you prefer that we not exchange your name with third parties, or if you wish to clarify or modify your communication preferences, please visit us at www.ReaderService.com/consumerschoice or write to us at Reader Service Preference Service, P.O. Box 9049, Buffalo, NY 14269-9049. Include your name and address.

50BFT19R

COMING NEXT MONTH FROM
Love Inspired®

Available August 19, 2019

SHELTER FROM THE STORM
North Country Amish • by Patricia Davids

Pregnant and unwed, Gemma Lapp's determined to return to her former home in Maine. After she misses her bus, the only way to get there is riding with her former crush, Jesse Crump. And when he learns her secret, he might just have a proposal that'll solve all her problems...

HER FORGOTTEN COWBOY
Cowboy Country • by Deb Kastner

After a car accident leaves Rebecca Hamilton with amnesia, the best way to recover her memory is by moving back to her ranch—with her estranged husband, whose unborn child she carries. As she rediscovers herself, can Rebecca and Tanner also reclaim their love and marriage?

THE BULL RIDER'S SECRET
Colorado Grooms • by Jill Lynn

Mackenzie Wilder isn't happy when her brother hires her ex-boyfriend, Jace Hawke, to help out on their family's guest ranch for the summer. Jace broke her heart when he left town without an explanation. But can he convince her he deserves a second chance?

REUNITED IN THE ROCKIES
Rocky Mountain Heroes • by Mindy Obenhaus

Stopping to help a pregnant stranded driver, police officer Jude Stephens comes face-to-face with the last person he expected—the woman he once loved. Now with both of them working on a local hotel's renovations, can Jude and Kayla Bradshaw overcome their past to build a future together?

A MOTHER FOR HIS TWINS
by Jill Weatherholt

First-grade teacher Joy Kelliher has two new students—twin little boys who belong to her high school sweetheart. And if teaching Nick Capello's sons wasn't enough, the widower's also her neighbor...and competing for the principal job she wants. Will little matchmakers bring about a reunion Joy never anticipated?

HOMETOWN HEALING
by Jennifer Slattery

Returning home with a baby in tow, Paige Cordell's determined her stay is only temporary. But to earn enough money to leave, she needs a job—and her only option is working at her first love's dinner theater. Now can Jed Gilbertson convince her to stay for good? _____

LICNM0819